# RORY

## PJ FIALA

ROLLING THUNDER PUBLISHING

## GET A FREE EBOOK!

Building a relationship with my readers is the very best thing about writing. I send monthly newsletters with details on new releases, special offers and other fun things relating to my books.

If you sign up to my mailing list I'll send you:

1. A copy of Moving to Love, Book 1 of the Rolling Thunder series.

2. A book list so you know what order to read my books in.

You can get Moving to Love **for free,** by signing up at https://landing.mailerlite.com/webforms/landing/n1o3i7

# DEDICATION

I've had so many wonderful people come into my life and I want you all to know how much I appreciate it. From each and every reader who takes the time out of their days to read my stories and leave reviews, thank you.

My beautiful, smart and fun Road Queens, who play games with me, post fun memes, keep the conversation rolling and help me create these captivating characters, places, businesses and more. Thank you ladies for your ideas, support and love. The following characters and places were created by:

Rory's nickname Ace - Melissa Hultz

Rory's siblings - Rory's siblings are Rochelle (sister) named by Jo West

Rourke (brother) and Rowan (sister) named by AnneMarie Dodds

Captain Jason (Jase) Peters - named by Kristi Hombs-Kopydlowski

Detective Callan Waters - named by Annemieke Westerbeek

Detective Samuel Bowers - named by Nicky Ortiz

Officer Anderson (Ty) Tyler - named by Cynthia Reifel
Officer Paul Delhurst - named by Debbie Douglas-Moncrief
Alice's partner in Indy - Ben Michaels - named by Annemieke Westerbeek
Informants: Twitch; ringtone "Close To My Enemies" by Kalado - named by Lisa Martin
Pigeon; Ringtone Friends in Low Places - named by Nicky Ortiz and Patricia Case
Realtor - Margery Van Steel of Van Steel Realty - named by Kerry Harteker
Rush Trucking - Owner Geoff Rush - named by Nicky Ortiz and Lynda Gettier
Harley was created and named by Karen Hawk, Kristi Hombs Kopydlowski, Kerry Harteker, Kim Ruiz and Val Clarizio.

A special thank you to Marijane Diodati, my amazing editor and Teresa Ellett Russ, my PR assistant.
Thank you to Becky McGraw of Cover Me Photography and Design for the amazing cover. It all comes together because of these exceptional ladies.

Last but not least, my family for the love and sacrifices they have made and continue to make to help me achieve this dream, especially my husband and best friend, Gene. Words can never express how much you mean to me.

To our veterans and current serving members of our armed forces, police and fire departments, thank you ladies and gentlemen for your hard work and sacrifices; it's with gratitude and thankfulness that I mention you in this forward.

# COPYRIGHT

Printed in the United States of America
    First published 2020
    Fiala, PJ
    Rory:Finding His Match / PJ Fiala
    p. cm.
    1.   Romance—Fiction.  2.   Romance—Suspense.  3.
Romance - Military
    I. Title – Rory:Finding His Match

# ALSO BY PJ FIALA

Click here to see a list of all of my books with the blurbs.

**Contemporary Romance**

**Rolling Thunder Series**

Moving to Love, Book 1

Moving to Hope, Book 2

Moving to Forever, Book 3

Moving to Desire, Book 4

Moving to You, Book 5

Moving Home, Book 6

**Second Chances Series**

Designing Samantha's Love, Book 1

Securing Kiera's Love, Book 2

**Military Romantic Suspense**

**Bluegrass Security Series**

Heart Thief, Book One

Finish Line, Book Two

Lethal Love, Book Three

**Big 3 Security**

Ford: Finding His Fire Book One

Lincoln: Finding His Mark Book Two

Dodge: Finding His Jewel Book Three

Rory: Finding His Match Book Four

**GHOST**

**1**

——————

Driving through the eastern side of town, dog-ass tired and ready for bed, Rory glanced over at the gas station parking lot as he neared the intersection. Suspicious of what looked like a drug deal going down, he quickly turned into the lot directing his headlights at two men exchanging a tiny bag for money.

Stopping, close to the men near the convenience store, Rory exited his vehicle and began walking toward them when they took off running in different directions. Choosing to follow the man who'd taken the money, he kept pace the best he could; but he was losing ground to the spry, lanky drug dealer, who was likely scared and surely not interested in spending the night in jail.

He was likely a low-level dealer, but with enough pressure sometimes these guys gave up a higher-up or two.

A gunshot rang out, then another. Diving behind a dumpster, which provided some cover, but likely not enough, he glanced around the side in the direction of the shots. His heartbeat quickened, but luckily his senses seemed to intensify as the adrenaline pumped through his body.

Seeing the flash of dark clothing duck behind the Longstone Apartment building before him, he crouched low and squat-walked to the side of the building, then slowly moved in the direction of his perp. His gun was out and pointed before him, when his ears heard a slight crunching of feet on gravel. Slowly raising himself up, he pointed his gun toward the corner of the building and sent up a quick prayer to be spot-on today. No accidents.

A gunshot sounded, and a bullet hit the building about a foot above his head from the direction his perp had run. Quickly dropping to the ground, he slowly let out a breath, inhaled again and scrambled to the edge of the second apartment building, adjacent to Longstone, which he thought was the direction of the shot.

Standing quickly and twisting his body so he was leading with his right hand holding his gun, he moved around the building, the brick walls scratching his back as he hovered close.

Movement from the shadows just a couple of feet in front of him and a flash of metal aimed at his head had him leveling his gun back at this new target.

"DEA." She half-whispered, half-yelled. Her voice was tight, her emotions likely as high as his.

"Lynyrd Station PD." He responded. Then wondered where in the hell a DEA Special Agent had come from and why. Lynyrd Station PD didn't have the luxury of a DEA agent's help.

They stood for a few seconds, each assessing the other, guns leveled on the other, emotions still high.

She stepped into the sliver of light that shone from the overhead streetlights and he damned near dropped his weapon. Familiar eyes stared back at him, the hypnotic green he remembered from years ago. Before he'd left the Marines. Before he'd been married to Debra.

He watched those mesmerizing eyes change as she recognized him, then worried that the emotion he saw in them was more hatred than friendliness or happiness, his heart hammered once more in his chest.

"Beggs, what the fuck are you doing here?" he snapped.

"I'm chasing a lead, the same as you I suspect."

A bullet hit the corner of the building they now stood alongside of and pieces of brick rained down on him. His instinct to protect took over and he wrapped his arm around Beggs and shoved her against the wall, shielding her with his body.

He turned then to give chase, but Beggs shoved him out of the way. "Asshole."

T hen she took off running to yet another apartment building across the alley, small expanse of lawn which served as the apartment complexes' green space and was surrounded by four three story apartment buildings, then she disappeared under the stairwell. Giving pursuit he followed in her wake but was met with more shooting then nothing but silence. Hiding under a stairwell, trying to catch his breath, and forcing his brain to catch up with events, he slightly shook his head and listened. Nothing.

Venturing out from his hiding spot he looked around for Beggs but didn't see the direction she'd gone or the perp they'd been following after the last shot. Ugly doubts crawled through his brain that he was ineffective at his job as he heaved himself off the wall he'd pressed himself against and quietly turned the corner, which led him back to the gas station where it'd all began this evening.

A cruiser had pulled up behind his car, and another was just now racing toward the station. Recognizing the officer interviewing two witnesses he walked toward them, all the while chastising himself for getting a tad out of shape and unable to chase a doper, even though he was only 42 now. The guys would likely have a bit of fun with him this week, but that he could take, he'd given his share over the years.

"Richards." One of the newly arrived officers, Anderson Tyler, walked toward him, his strides long and his gait determined.

"Ty, what do you have?"

"Calls coming into the station, gunshots hitting buildings, tenants in the apartments are scared and sick of the crime, the station is going nuts. Then someone calls in your plates and says they saw you running after someone. Needless to say, the Captain isn't happy; you went in without backup and we have more unhappy citizens. What do you have?"

He took a deep breath and looked into Ty's tired eyes. They'd all been putting in sixty to eighty hours a week recently and it was taking its toll on all of them.

"I came into the parking lot because I was pretty sure I saw a drug deal going down. Took off on foot to chase the dealer and ran into a DEA Special Agent. Anything at the station on that?"

The big man shook his head. He was easily six foot two or more, but his broad shoulders and massive arms made him appear larger than life.

"Nothing. Ask the Captain. " He pointed to the other

officer, Jerry Robards, and said, "I'll go help Jerry interview witnesses. The Captain wants to see you."

"Yeah. I bet he does."

He let out a long breath and dragged his sorry, tired ass to his car. Captain Jason Peters was a great boss, low key, knowledgeable and easy to deal with. Unless he was pissed off. Then, he could chew on your ass for hours and not show signs of getting tired. Rory feared that's what was about to happen, and quite frankly, he was too fucking exhausted to have his ass chewed on. It was a recipe for disaster. And where in the fuck did Beggs go? That was something he'd not been able to wrap his mind around and he didn't know how to get in touch with her, either. But she'd said, DEA, so he would start with the Chicago DEA Division. Indiana was one of three states in that Division. To be here she likely was stationed at a DEA Office in one of them.

## 2

F ucking Rory Richards. Doesn't that just beat the shit out of a dead dog? Flipping irritating. Bastard never called her even though he'd promised he would. They'd dated for over two months then she was transferred to a different base in Arizona and he stayed in South Carolina. The first week, she thought he was just busy and so was she, going through the new paperwork and learning all the new faces and places. But then the second week rolled around and no call, then the third. She kept herself busy with duties on base and even went so far as to volunteer for a couple of extra duties to keep herself occupied. Then she realized he wasn't going to call, ever. Damned if she'd break down and call him, she had pride. Six months later she heard he'd married, and she went on a wild drunk with some battle-buddies, girl-friends she'd met on base and it took her a couple of days to actually sober out. Then, she put Rory Fucking Richards out of her mind and focused on her job.

And for all of that with Rory, she never thought to ask him where he was from and she never looked back to see where he ended up. Coming face-to-face with him last night was a shock to her system for sure. Though it was dark, he still had those same piercing blue eyes she remembered. That same dark hair and that presence. Oh, that's what rankled more than anything. Seeing him again stirred things in her.

Tossing her belongings into her overnight bag, she grabbed her shampoo and conditioner from the shower and threw them into the baggies she always packed them in, then into the bag with the rest of her stuff, she was ready. One more quick look around and she was satisfied she could go back home to Indianapolis and forget, once again, Rory Fucking Richards.

Hefting her overnight bag over her shoulder, she picked up the checkout notice that had been pushed under her door, then folded it neatly and tucked it in the side pouch of her bag to make sure she turned it into the Office for reimbursement when she got back. Opening the door, the cool, crisp fall air woke her up like nothing else could, except for that cup of coffee she was dying for. The diner connected to the motel she was staying at would no doubt have it; though it was likely not to the caliber she was used to, she'd take it. It always took two or three cups for her to get her bearings in the morning.

Walking down the sidewalk to the diner, she opened the door and was hit with the warmth of the room and the aroma of bacon and eggs. Her stomach rumbled, but she had no intention of staying any longer than she needed to. Her lead from her informant last night was nothing more than a setup and she was particularly pissed off that he'd double-crossed her. She'd deal with him when she got back, too.

"Can I help you?"

A pretty young waitress with bright, shiny eyes and long blond hair, pulled back into a ponytail, asked her.

"Ah, yes, coffee. Black. In a to-go cup, please."

"You got it." The perky gal said as she immediately turned to begin filling up a paper cup.

Pulling a five dollar bill from her wallet inside her purse, she lay it on the counter and watched as the young lady continued to fill her cup, set the plastic white top on it and checked it to make sure it was secure. Turning toward her, she set her cup on the counter, smiled and asked, "Did you want anything to go with it? Our special this morning is a bagel, cream cheese and a side of bacon for $3.00.

"That sounds delicious, but I don't eat breakfast until around ten o'clock; I need my coffee first. Thank you though." She picked up her coffee, then said, "Keep the change." And headed toward the door.

Opening her car door and setting her cup in the console, she reached around the driver's seat, dropped her bag into the backseat, then settled in for her 170-mile trip back to Indy.

Starting her car and pulling out of her space, her phone rang, and she said, "Answer call."

A beep sounded. "Tucker," she answered.

"Al, I've got a job for you. The Lynyrd Station PD just asked for assistance from DEA. They're dealing with a mighty drug issue and since you're in town, I told them to expect you this morning. You'll be there until you can help them solve this problem. I think it mirrors our case in that the drugs filtering into Lynyrd Station are likely coming from that dealer and supplier you've been trying to nab."

" I know you're the Special Agent in Charge, Ben, but

please, no. I don't want to be out of the Office again so soon."

"No one does, Al, but you're needed and you're there. This is what we do. Offices like ours, even in a city the size of Indy, don't just get to handle the inner-city cases like drug gangs. Al, you know all of us are tasked to help rural areas that can't afford to handle these drug cases or don't have the people they need. Keep me updated."

Rubbing her forehead with her fingers, she stifled the litany of colorful words at the ready and remembered that this was her SAC she was talking to. Lifting her coffee from the center console she thought perhaps she needed to get caffeinated and soon. Drinking as much as she could due to the temperature of the coffee, she silently waited her boss out.

"Al, I know you're seething right now. I wouldn't ask if the Chicago Office didn't order it. And, since you'll be up for promotion next month, which will keep you home more, it's important that you do this. And, shut that drug operation down."

"Yeah. Got it." She'd better get that damned promotion this time. Last time they gave it to that whiner, Steiner. He was a pain in the ass for certain.

"Thanks, Al, be nice."

"Yeah."

She ended the call without another word, then took a couple of deep breaths, turned around in the parking lot, and headed back to Lynyrd Station and the police department, where she'd no doubt run into Rory again. Today was really beginning to blow.

# 3

Dragging his feet into the station, he hadn't even bothered to put his jacket on this morning, opting for carrying it in case he needed it. Lack of sleep and thoughts of Beggs filtered through his mind all night. He should have called her all those years ago when she'd left, it was a young dumb-ass thing to do. But he'd found out the day after she left that she could have stayed. All it would have taken was a word from her to her commanding officer. She chose to leave, which he took as wanting to get away from him. But he didn't want to settle down anyway, and at the time and they were on opposite coasts. Long-distance didn't make sense then. He'd gone out three days in a row after she left to drink her away. One week turned into two and then he met Debra. At first, they were just having fun. She'd been like Beggs in that she gave him shit when he needed it and she was strong and confident. That was his kryptonite. Strong women when they needed to be, saucy in bed.

Flopping into his desk chair, he rested his elbows on the desk and swiped his fingers down his face.

"Long night?"

Removing his hands and looking at the man speaking, he sighed at Captain Jason Peters. "Yeah, Captain. A lot of them lately."

"Well, then I have good news. DEA is sending us some help. I guess some hotshot Special Agent from Indianapolis named Al Tucker. All I know is Tucker is good and we need the help."

Sitting back hard in his chair he looked his Captain in the eye. "I don't know if that's good news, Cap. I'm dog-ass tired, we all are, and training a new guy on our procedures and town sounds like a monumental task right now."

Captain nodded. "Maybe it'll only be a day or two, then Tucker should be up to speed. This is the first time we've worked with DEA, but they help police departments like ours all the time. The sooner we get these drugs off the street, the sooner we can stop burying our town's children. I've been to my share of funerals these days."

"Yeah." The feeling of defeat fell over him like a wet coat. More hours and now a "hotshot", which to his ears sounded like a cocky, self-centered bastard.

The Captain left his doorway and he shook his mouse to wake up his computer. Starting with the DEA Chicago Division database he wanted to satisfy himself that Beggs was far, far away hopefully in Chicago. He typed in her name Alice Beggs and half-assed chuckled. He'd only called her Alice once while they'd been together, always referring to her as either Beggs or Red.

He watched the little circle turn as it searched. Then, the chatter outside of his office stopped. Eerie silence fell as all eyes were trained toward the front door. Curiosity got the better of him. He stood and made his way to the door of his office and looked in the direction of all the other detectives.

There she was. Beggs. Her shiny red hair spilled over her shoulders in waves. The freckles that were abundant on her face seemed to stand out more just now, he'd always thought they were cute. Then, her intense green eyes looked up and focused on him. He felt it. The minute she realized he was watching her. Her eyes bore into his and the beginnings of a grin formed on his face, then her eyes narrowed and the look she leveled on him would have made a boner droop. She was not happy to see him.

It took his brain a few minutes to grasp the situation, and if he thought he could have run and hid in his office, he would have; but then she began moving toward him and his damned feet betrayed him and refused to move. He felt like a deer with his eyes caught in the headlights and his brain sent off warning signals that this was not going to be good. But there he stood anyway.

She stopped just in front of him, her eyes no longer squinting but the stiffness in her face said she was not happy.

"Special Agent Al Tucker at your service." Her smooth sexy voice floated over him and his brain screamed, "NO!"

"Al? Tucker? You're Al Tucker?"

"Problem with that?"

"No. It's just I thought your name was Beggs."

She inhaled deeply and let it out slowly. The fresh aroma of coffee swirled around, and he watched as she took a drink from the paper cup in her hand.

"My married name is Tucker. My first name, as you know, is Alice. I go by Al to my friends."

Swallowing the large lump in his throat, he heard

snickering around him and knew he was going to have to answer a ton of questions this week.

Nodding once, he said, "Nice to see you again, Al."

"Alice."

"I thought you said Al..."

"I said my friends call me Al. You. Are. Not. My. Friend."

That earned her chuckles from the men sitting around observing this interaction and she bestowed a fantastic smile on them.

"Right. Well, please come into my office and we'll go over the information we have on file with this drug problem."

He stood back a step to let her pass, but she cocked her head and waited for him to move in front of her. Feeling sheepish and knowing the guys were all watching, he took her cue and preceded her into his office. Walking around the desk to sit in his chair, he waited for her to sit down as he pulled a couple of the files he'd been working on out of his desk drawer. Remembering his search, he quickly minimized his screen and was relieved to see her head had been down as she looked at the chairs.

Laying the files on the top of the desk, he watched as she leaned forward, her long trench coat still cinched at her narrow waist, her body still slender, her long fingers still caught his attention as she opened the first file and began reading his reports.

"I'm sorry. I should have called. Or I shouldn't have promised to call, however you have decided to look at it."

Her eyes flicked to his and held. His stomach knotted but he waited for her.

"I guess it worked out for both of us the way it was supposed to. I heard you got married."

He squirmed in his chair a bit, then cleared his throat. "Yes. But I'm widowed now."

He saw an emotion flicker across her face, then she swallowed, her soft voice came back. "I'm sorry."

Nodding he ventured further. "How long have you been married?"

"Four years."

His eyes flicked to her ring finger. Not only was there not a ring there, there wasn't an indentation either. Curious.

"Tell me what we have going on here so I can go home."

# 4

---

Sitting in this small office, she could smell him. That same after shave, after all these damned years, she'd never forget it. They hadn't dated that long, just a couple of months, but he'd left a mark on her. More than just the hurt at how he had forgotten about her. More than his scent. She sat here now, listening to his voice and her body responded. Her nipples puckered and when he glanced up to see if she were listening, he'd smiled a couple of times and dammit, that had an effect on her.

"Tell me what questions you have." She looked up to see him watching her.

Clearing her throat lightly, she flipped the file on top to another section. "So, if I'm clear on all of this, you've had two kids die in the past couple of weeks of overdoses and one of a gunshot which you believe to be part of a drug deal gone wrong. Then we have the events of last night. This is escalating."

"Yes. We had a crime family move into town last year and set up business, the Santarinos. Not only were they smuggling illegal weapons, they were art and jewel smug-glers and thieves. We suspected they were involved with bringing in drugs, but we didn't confirm it until around the time the family's legitimate business was taken down and the brothers, Victor and Mangus, who ran the legiti-mate and illegal operations were dead. The family is gone now. Sofia Santarino, who lives in Italy, and is Mangus' widow who still owns the property in Lynyrd Station, where Limitless International, the legitimate business was located, before law enforcement shut it down. We thought we were done with the Santarinos, but now we've got this issue going on and I can't help but wonder if they had something in the works before they died. Someone is still bringing drugs into the area and distributing. We've been watching all known employees of their legitimate company, Limitless International, as well as all known cohorts of the Santarinos. So far we can't pin anything on them."

He flipped the page in the file and photographs, stacked neatly and clipped into the folder came into view. "This is Mangus Santarino and this is his brother, Victor."

He continued flipping pictures, his thick masculine hands mesmerized her. "This is Giovanni Santarino, their father. He's in his nineties now, living in Italy, not sure of his health. It's doubtful he has anything to do with the drugs here, though he could carry a grudge since both sons died in Lynyrd Station. But we can't get any informa-tion on whether he's capable of running the family over there. And this is Francesca Santarino, daughter of Mangus. She's in federal prison."

He flipped to another photograph. "This is Chibs, he was one of the black-market gun distributors. He's incar-cerated in federal prison now as well. And this is Xavier

Creed, also a gunrunner, also in federal prison. The only local not in prison is Butch Ariens who owns a pawn shop, Black Gold Pawn, in town. He was the middleman exchanging money for art, jewels or drugs to work off a debt he owed the Santarinos. He left town and the shop is closed."

"Okay. So, of these men you have in your file, do any of them have family who would take up the job of running drugs?"

"We're checking into everyone, but we don't have the resources to watch all of them, hence here you are! And speaking of, how is it we weren't informed until this morning that you were coming and yet you happened to be here last night? And, why were you here last night?"

She sat back, her coffee cup now empty and she needed another one. The beginnings of a headache were starting as she sat here fighting her attraction to Rory and trying to process the info dump that she just went through. Trying to decide how much she should tell him, she felt exhausted already.

"I was here on a lead I got from an informant. I'm thinking he has more information than he let on and I believe it was a bit of a setup last night. I got an email this morning from another agent that while I was here chasing my target, which by the way, you screwed up for me, a major drug deal went down back home. Then, this morning as I was packing to leave, my SAC called to tell me you needed an agent and since I was already here, I'm now stuck here, literally."

"I didn't screw up your bust last night."

"Really?" She leaned forward and locked eyes with him. "What the fuck do you call tossing me against the building and blocking my view to his direction?"

"I didn't toss...."

The instant he faltered, she stood, "Where's the coffee here?"

He shook his head quickly as if to clear his thoughts, then stood and walked toward her. "I'll show you the coffee and introduce you to the guys."

He stopped just before her and held his hand out as if to tell her to go on ahead of him. She pulled her trench coat off and lay it in her vacant chair. She walked in front of him because she wasn't as pissed as she had been, and she rather liked keeping him off-kilter. One time she wouldn't precede him, another she would. She might as well have a little fun while she was here. Stepping out into the work area, she saw a couple of the guys stop and look up from their computers.

Rory stepped out from behind her and a couple of the men grinned shit-ass eating grins, which in her experience working mostly with men, told her they thought she chewed his ass out but good and they couldn't wait to get the rest of the story. That could be fun, too.

"Coffee's over here."

She followed him as he turned left and around a corner. There was a small galley kitchen with barely enough room for both of them, so she warned herself not to get too close, but the aroma of fresh coffee, even police station coffee, sent her thoughts racing to the need for another cup.

Rory walked to the coffee machine, and she watch the muscles in his broad shoulders move and bunch as he reached up into a cupboard to pull two clean coffee cups down. They were Styrofoam but still clean. He looked over his shoulder as he poured, "Still take yours black?"

Her heartbeat kicked up. "You remember how I take my coffee?"

He froze, the coffee pot mid-air before beginning to pour again. It was brief, but noticeable. "Yeah, I guess I do."

"What else do you remember?" Dumb, dumb, dumb. Why in the hell did her mouth say that?

He set the pot on the burner, reached into the cupboard for lids for each cup, snapped them on the cups, then turned to hand her a cup before answering. Her heartbeat kicked up ten beats per minute waiting for his answer. It seemed important for some reason. He looked her in the eyes, those light blue orbs she'd fallen for so flipping long ago, were still beautiful. Intelligent and captivating. The dark lashes that matched his dark hair were thick and full, giving his eyes the most envious frame. He waited a few beats before responding.

"I remember everything."

Angry with herself for loving that answer, she snapped, "Except to call."

She turned and stormed from the room and headed to the detectives who seemed interested in what was happening in the kitchen.

## 5

---

He'd been silently beating himself up about why he didn't stay in contact with her when she'd been transferred. Why he didn't try harder to have a long-distance relationship with her? Life may have been so different if he had. Of course, it would have, it would have been worlds apart from his lonely life here. But, just then, that snap of anger and sass that popped out of her mouth, reminded him of why, at least one reason why. When they were so much younger, he'd had this strange feeling that she'd run right over him. That all of his life he'd be cow-towing to her. She'd had a temper; it had come in spurts and dissipated almost as quickly as it had started. And, as a young twenty-year-old, he wondered about marriage. But it seemed like there was so much life left to live single. Then he found out she could have stayed, and his hurt feelings and pride told him to move on. If she wanted to be with him, she would have tried to work it out. Note to self, steer clear of Alice Beggs Tucker, 'cause now, he found himself excited about her sass. He enjoyed her confidence.

Exiting the kitchen, his gut knotted when he entered the detective work area and there she was, her red hair shining in the sunlight from the window, shaking hands with each of the guys he worked with. By the looks of them she was enchanting each of them and for some reason that irritated the shit out of him.

"Well, it's very nice to meet you Detective Sam. I'm sure we'll be working together while I'm here." Her smoky voice flitted through the air and all the men seemed captivated by her.

"Nice meeting you to, Al." Samuel Bowers, looked up at him with the biggest fucking grin on his face and he knew what that was about. She'd told them all they could call her Al. But he wasn't her friend. He'd see about that.

Taking a drink of his coffee, he walked past the group of them and snipped, "When you and your friends are finished wasting time, we need a task meeting to discuss what each of us knows about the murder last week and the other open cases of the past two months, where these drugs are coming from and the progress we've made. I'll be in the conference room."

Probably a bit childish. Probably a bit unprofessional. But he'd had three hours of sleep last night and not much more the previous couple of weeks and he wasn't in the mood. At all.

Turning the corner, he stopped in his office to grab his files, then exited and went to the conference room just two doors down.

Setting his files on the conference room table, he set his coffee down, pulled out the chair at the head of the table and sat down. Opening his files, he pretended to be reading but he was mentally chastising himself for letting his feelings get in the way of his work. He wasn't going to get involved with Beggs again anyway, besides, she's married, so it didn't matter if she thought he was her friend. His goal was the same today as yesterday, solve the murder and get the drugs off the street. If she could help with the drugs, perfect.

"Everything alright?"

He looked up to see Detective Callan Waters enter the room, his always perceptive gaze scrutinizing everything and right now he was looking closely at him.

"Yeah. A bit of a history in case you couldn't tell. Ended badly. This is going to be tough."

Cal pulled the chair next to him away from the table and sat down. He was a big brawny man and the ladies usually swooned when Cal walked in the room. More than once, he begrudgingly used Cal to get an uncooperative female suspect chatting. They loved his attention and he was fantastic at making them feel like he was on their side.

"Yeah, it's a tad noticeable."

Before he could say anything more, Sam Bowers, Anderson Tyler and Alice entered the room. Their chatter subsided and they quickly took their seats.

"Okay, let's start with the murder of Justin Tully. Ty, you were handling that case, fill us in."

Ty opened the file in front of him and just as Ty opened his mouth to start, Rory's phone rang. Reaching for it, Rory saw the readout said "Captain". Holding his finger up to let them know he had to take this, he tapped the answer icon on his phone.

"Captain, how can I help you?"

"Rory, we found a body behind building B at the apartment complex where you were chasing your perp last night. Bring a team with you, this is a bloody mess."

"For fuck's sake, what in the hell is going on here?" Remembering who he was speaking to, he continued. "We'll be right there."

Quickly standing, he said, "This has to wait, we have a dead body and it's a mess. Let's go, all hands-on deck."

Files closed and chairs rolled back as they all stood and headed to the door. He left before all of them eager to get to the scene and see what they were dealing with. Not really eager, it sounded a fright, but maybe this one would lead them to the information they needed to figure this shit out.

"Mind if I ride with you, Ace?"

He turned to see Alice staring at him her face serious, her posture straight and tall. She'd always been gorgeous, but just now, with dark-blue dress slacks and a nice white blouse, her red hair flowing over her shoulders, she was stunning. She scooped her trench coat from the chair in his office where she'd left it, he was irritated that she'd called him by the nickname she'd given him oh so many years ago.

"Sure." He walked past her and headed to the back-door. She wore sensible shoes, but he could hear them behind him, not exactly trying to keep up, but in a hurry.

Pushing the backdoor open he didn't bother to hold it for her. He decided anger was a bit of what he needed at the moment to keep his mind on the task at hand.

As he neared his cool sleek black Charger, he smiled. He always did when he looked at this car. It had been his dream for a long time, and he loved every minute of owning it. Using the fob in his hand he tapped the unlock button and smiled again as the car lit up, taillights, dome light inside. She was a thing of beauty.

"Fantastic car, Rory. For some reason I pegged you as a truck kinda guy."

Opening his door, he sarcastically said, "That wouldn't be the first time you've pegged me wrong, Beggs."

## 6

----

The drive was quiet. Too quiet.

"Look, I'm sorry I hurt your feelings. But you hurt mine."

His head turned and she could see his jaw clench. Those piercing blue eyes landed on her and held, then he shook his head and looked at the road.

"And how's that?"

Taking in a deep breath, she swallowed. Knowing this conversation would come up, but not at all ready to hear that she'd been easily forgotten, she forged on.

"I was transferred to another base. You said you'd call and we'd stay in touch. You didn't. We didn't. Then, within six months you were married to someone else." She stared straight ahead, watching as the trees and shrubs breezed past the windows of the car. The sun was now high in the sky and the day seemed bright, though the air was chilly. It didn't seem possible that they were on their way to a gruesome murder scene.

"We were young."

"You still married someone else."

She watched his chest, which all these years later, was massively impressive. He'd continued to work out after getting out of the Marines. He'd always been impressive, but now, he was filled out and mature. He had a confidence about him he hadn't had back when they were stationed together.

"You could have stayed, Alice, but you didn't. I heard the position you took was volunteer, you could have refused."

"But then I'd be staying in a place, career wise, that didn't offer me the opportunities I got when I left."

His jaw clenched again but instead of answering, he turned into the apartment complex parking lot where they'd first seen each other last night. The place was teaming with police cruisers, an ambulance, the medical examiner's van and on-lookers standing behind the yellow police tape trying to see what was happening. A news truck was parked in the corner, the large antennas raised high and a reporter with long dark hair and a cute little cream-colored pea coat could be seen talking into the camera pointed in her direction.

Rory drove to a parking area blocked off for police personnel, a young officer guarding the area from unauthorized persons stepped aside when Rory pulled up, a smile on his face. He clearly admired the sleek black Charger as they rolled past him. Pulling in next to a cruiser, he put the car in Park, turned it off, and grabbed his keys from the ignition. Without another word, he opened his car door and exited the vehicle.

Taking in a deep, cleansing breath, first, because she didn't have the patience to deal with a surly co-worker, and second, because once they got close to the body, there would be no clean breaths for a while.

Opening the car door and exiting, the doors locked, and she saw Rory pointing the key fob at the car, then turn and walked to an officer on the fringe of the roped off area.

Following Rory's path, she heard the officer as he pointed to an area behind him. "The Captain's between those two buildings. Medical Examiner is there, too."

Al moved on past them to the area the officer had mentioned, stealing herself for the scene. She hated looking at dead bodies. Sometimes it took a while to get the images out of her head and to erase the smells from her memories.

Refusing to wear high heels, even in dress clothes, she was once again grateful for what some would call sensible shoes, as she plodded across the uneven ground easily in her high-topped sneaker type shoes. Nearing the corner of the building the odor of death hit her before she saw anything, and she quickly pulled a scarf from her coat pocket to cover her nose and mouth should she begin to gag.

The scene that met her when she turned the corner was primarily the backs of a large man and a smaller man talking and pointing. As she stepped close to them, she finally made herself look at the ground. A male body lay on the ground, his face covered in blood, blank eyes staring up at the sky. One of his arms lay across his stomach, one lay out at a 45-degree angle. A red blob lay next to his face, in a pool of blood.

She heard Rory's steps quicken as she stared at the body on the ground, and then the steps of others as they neared the scene. There was an area marked off for them where the forensic technicians had already collected evidence, documented what they found, and taken photographs. They were now photographing the area around them, taking notes, and continuing to gather evidence. No one was permitted on the part of the scene that had not been processed.

"Captain, this is Al Tucker." Rory introduced her. The taller of the two men turned to look at her, reached his hand out to shake hers, then motioned to the man alongside him.

"This is Medical Examiner Thomson."

The Medical Examiner nodded at her. "What do you have for us?", Alice asked.

"His throat was slit from jaw to jaw, and his tongue cut out."

She looked at the blob lying next to his face, then looked closer at the face staring up. The word snitch was carved into his forehead.

The Medical Examiner pointed to a forensic technician's evidence tote where she could see evidence paraphernalia and plastic bags containing various evidence. "A wallet found on the victim identifies him as Sergio Mancuoso."

Her head snapped up as she stared at the Medical Examiner. But at that moment, her stomach quelled, and she stepped back in case she lost the coffee she'd consumed earlier. Rory followed her a few steps back.

"Do you know him?"

Breathing in slow and deep and letting her breath out slowly, she swallowed the moisture that had gathered in her mouth. Her heart hammered in her chest as her mind reeled with what this might mean. The only thing that came to mind right now was that she might very well be in more danger than she's ever been at this juncture, and she needed some time to think and call her SAC for his thoughts on the matter.

"Beggs? Do you know him?" Rory asked again.

She looked into his concerned face and, for the first time since last night, she was happy he was here.

"Yes."

"Who is he to you?"

"He's my informant. The instant I got to this spot last night, which is where he told me I'd find a major drug drop going down and possibly one of the organizers, 'The Big Guy' of this drug operation I've been trying to shut down, I was shot at. I thought he set me up because back home in Indianapolis there was a major bust last night. When I found out about it, I assumed he wanted me out of the area so I wouldn't break it up, and then have me killed because someone was waiting for me. But he didn't set me up, he was found out."

"Are you in danger, Beggs?"

He watched her face and the myriad of emotions that flashed across it. The slight furrow between her brows told him she was worried.

"I don't know, but they may have gotten him to talk. It would explain why I was being shot at last night. I thought I'd gotten too close."

"Why were you here without backup?" He was

bouncing between being pissed and being scared at her willingness to put herself in danger.

"I wanted to sneak up on the drug drop and record it so I had evidence. I wasn't going to bust anyone until I had recorded evidence and names. This case has been getting to me. I've spent countless hours researching, investigating, examining and I keep coming up with nothing. I realize I shouldn't have come alone, but my partner was working another angle at home.

"You still put yourself in dang..." Seeing her shut down, he stopped his forthcoming tirade and changed his tone of voice.

He took a deep breath and let it out slowly. "I think we need to get you to safety right now until we get the evidence back at the station and we know if your snitch gave the killers details about you. What did he know about you? How did he contact you?"

"He only knew my phone number and that I worked in Indianapolis."

"And that you were going to be here last night."

Her voice softened. "Yes."

"What did he call you?"

"Why does that matter?"

His gut twisted in several directions. The killing was getting more gruesome and now it felt very personal.

"I don't know."

"He called me sneakers."

Watching as she raised her pant leg, her sensible shoes were Rag & Bone Army high top sneakers. He had a pair of his own.

Inhaling deeply, he felt relief for some strange reason that he hadn't called her Red. Which, considering what they were facing, was stupid.

He looked back at the Captain, who was now approaching them, the look of confusion clear on his face.

"Everything alright here?"

He looked at Beggs but it appeared she wasn't going to say anything, so he did. "That's Beggs' informant."

Captain Peters was a large man, 6 foot 3 and he was muscular. Built like a brick shithouse should have his name on it in the dictionary, 'cause he was a solid wall of strength, both physically and mentally. His jet-black hair and dark chocolate eyes, which normally were serious now looked worried.

"Are you in danger, Tucker?"

Beggs cleared her throat lightly, squared her shoulders and looked Captain Peters in the eyes, which wasn't that easy to do, she had to look up close to a foot.

"I don't know, sir."

The Captain stared at Beggs for a long time and to her credit, she never looked away.

"Richards, get Tucker back to the station and figure out where she's going to stay while she's here. The motel isn't safe enough."

"I can go back to Indy." She offered.

Captain shook his head. "Nope. We might be on to something. If they're here because you're here, we have them close. That's a far cry better than having them scatter. As long as they know you're still here, we have a better chance of catching these fuckers and that's what we're going to do. I'll call your SAC to see if he agrees with the plan."

The Captain started to walk away. "Richards, on second thought, your place is secured with the latest and greatest, isn't it? Take Tucker there."

What? No fucking way. This wasn't a good idea at all. "Captain, maybe we could..."

"Take her to your place and lockdown until we have this scene processed. I'll call you in a while."

Then his massive back was turned, and he walked back to the body and his crime scene investigators.

"He can't make me stay at your place. That is un-fuck-ing-real. Besides, likely unethical. And to top it off, how fucking dare he. He'll call my SAC." Beggs seethed, though quietly. The Captain couldn't hear her and if he could, he didn't acknowledge it.

Taking a deep breath, more to fortify himself than anything else against her quick temper. " Beggs, let's get you out of sight for right now, then we can talk about what to do."

She faced him and crossed her arms in front of her. Totally protective move. He lowered his voice and tried again.

"Hey, I know you feel irritated with the way things have worked out today, but let's get out of sight and settled in, at least for tonight, and then we can talk. I'll talk about anything you want to talk about and if you need to scream and yell, you can scream and yell at me. But, right now, we don't know there isn't a sniper somewhere with his sights set on you."

She shook her beautiful head quickly as if she just realized she was in danger, then nodded her head and uncrossed her arms. At least for now, the temper had subsided. Now if she took him up on his offer to scream and yell, he'd have to deal with it, but at least he knew that would come out of frustration, and not so much about him. Maybe.

He turned and began walking to his car, turning only

once to make sure she was following. After rounding the corner of the building at the apartment complex, he could see the crowd was still large and it made his stomach roll. Their perp could be in the crowd out there for all they knew. Or in one of the apartments above them. Everything was a crap shoot right now.

He heard a phone ring, it wasn't his ring tone, but he turned as he heard Beggs dig for her phone in her coat pocket.

"Tucker."

"Who is this?" she demanded.

He stopped to see why she had stopped, her eyes looking all around. Seeing the absolute fear on her face, he walked back the few steps and took her free hand, grateful she didn't fight or argue. Pulling her along, he hurried his pace.

"Come out so I can see you or are you too cowardly?"

He squeezed her hand and looked back at her.

"Don't taunt him," he whispered.

She shushed him with a quick shake of her head as she listened to the person on the other end of the phone. He could only hear one side of the conversation, but what he surmised from that was that the killer could see them and that meant he needed to get Beggs out of here and fast. He quickened his pace and continued to tug her along, though she slowed a couple of times.

"I'll find you. I will. I'll get you."

She practically hissed. "Oh, I won't kill you. I'd much rather watch them walk you into prison knowing what your life will be like in there. Death would be a blessing for you. I have no intention of blessing you."

## 8

S he allowed herself to be pulled along but only because her mind was moving in a thousand different directions, not the least of which was that a murderer or murderers was watching. What that also meant, was he or they knew for sure what she looked like, knew she was with Rory, and what he looked like. They were only minimally protected by the small police force in Lynyrd Station, but cops were killed all the time, so it was possibly a false hope that they were safe anywhere.

Rory walked her to the passenger side of his car and opened the door for her, almost pushing her inside. The fact that he seemed scared began to freak her out, but she focused on her breathing, one minute at a time. Maybe after a good stiff drink, she could calm down and focus her thoughts on what she knew about this operation and her safety moving forward. She thought about the number of times her life had been in danger as a DEA Special Agent. She could handle this. She didn't want to stay at Rory's, not forever anyway.

He slid into the driver's seat and locked the doors.

Immediately pulling his seatbelt on, he glanced over at her. "Buckle up, Red."

The inside of the car was warm and cozy, Rory's after-shave filled the air, he called her by his old nickname for her and she suddenly felt better. Pulling her seatbelt on, he started the car, its low rumble, a sexy growl that gave her goosebumps, as he pulled from their parking space.

The young officer who'd let them pass by, stepped aside once again, that same grin as before, on his face.

"He has a crush on your car."

Rory glanced up at the young officer and nodded. "So do I."

He then left the parking lot, tapped the Bluetooth button on his dash, and upon doing so, the robotic female voice asked him what he wanted; he said, "Call Ford Montgomery."

"Calling Ford Montgomery on cell," came her reply.

The phone rang only twice before a deep, smoky male voice answered, "Yeah."

Rory chuckled before responding, "I have a situation."

"Yeah."

"Are you on a mission?"

"No. I'm in town."

"I have DEA Special Agent Alice Tucker in my car, and we've been ordered by the Captain to stay at my house. We're not sure if she's in danger, her informant was just found dead."

A long pause left her wondering if they'd been disconnected before Ford responded, "That's some situation."

"Right," Rory turned onto another road, leading them out of town, she tried running all of the scenarios through her head about what had happened last night, but wasn't totally successful. "My security system is in place and good, but I wonder if you can give it a once over, beef it up if need be?"

A baby cried in the background and Ford muttered something under his breath. "Yeah. I've got to help Megan get Shelby settled first; it's my turn to get her down for nap time, but I can be down in an hour."

Rory laughed, "You really are domesticated."

"Fuck you." Then the line went dead and Rory laughed again.

Turning into a cul-de-sac, she saw five larger homes each one spread out on close to two acres.

"This is beautiful."

Swinging the car into the driveway at one of the homes at the bottom of the cul-de-sac, the closest garage door of the three doors to the front door of the house began to open. The home was large; dark brown siding and stacked stone detailing at various places on the front of the home were stunning. The two-story home was tall and long and impressively sat perched on a hill. A true showpiece among the other homes.

"How does a cop afford this?" she murmured.

He didn't respond and she wondered if he'd turned dirty. Pulling the Charger into the garage, she noted that everything was neat and orderly. The walls were drywalled and painted white, the space organized with cabinets painted black along the back wall and nothing on the countertop except a picture of Rory's Charger and a Mopar sign.

"I have to tell you I'm impressed," she softly offered.

Turning off the ignition, he pulled the key out and opened his door. The look he landed on her was one of curiosity more than anything else. His words belied his look. "Glad you approve."

She exited the vehicle and followed him to a door which he unlocked. Stepping just inside the door he pushed a few buttons on a keypad, likely to turn off the alarm, paused for a moment, then a beep sounded, and he stood back and looked at her.

"Welcome to my home."

She stepped inside and the air felt warm and cozy, the faint aroma of citrus or something fresh filled the air. She followed Rory down the short hallway and to the right where they entered an impressive kitchen. Granite counters, oak cabinetry and tile floors looked out onto a large backyard. A small basket, filled with dog toys, lay on the floor next to the sliding glass doors leading to the backyard.

"You have a dog, Ace?"

His eyes landed on hers and held for a few moments as if he were trying to decide how to respond.

"I used to, but he died last year of cancer. I'd like another one but trying to train a puppy with the hours I've been working would be next to impossible right now, so I'm waiting to see how things shake out."

"I'm sorry you lost your dog, that sucks."

She watched his chest as it expanded, filling his lungs with air. He was still a handsome man, though his build was more on the stocky side, the way he'd filled out over these past few years was sexy. His dark hair showed tiny threads of silver here and there, mostly at the temples and behind his ears. He'd be handsome gray, too. His light blue eyes still cast a spell on her, the blue so unusual and clear like no other color she'd ever seen before.

"Yeah, it sucks." He opened a cupboard above a short counter across from the island and hung his keys on a peg.

"Come on, I'll show you your room."

She followed him, wondering how she'd get her car here which held all of the clothes she'd brought along with her, which really wasn't that much because she'd only expected to stay a day or two. While she would never describe herself as the average woman, she was when it came to packing. You just never knew when you needed to dress for a dinner or a change of clothes, in her case in the event she got filthy giving chase.

Rory walked through the open concept living room and turned left to ascend a large staircase. She silently followed him, wondering once again how he could afford this home. Cops usually lived modestly.

At the top of the steps, she looked out the large bank of windows onto the backyard and was enamored with the view, the decor, the entire home.

"Okay, take your pick of bedrooms, you have two to choose from and the bathroom is in the middle here. The entire upstairs is yours while you're here. I'll go down and call the station to have someone bring your car around and then I'll make us some lunch. Feel free to wash up. If you need clean clothes until yours get here, I can pull a t-shirt and some sweats from my room if you like."

She cleared her throat. "No, that's okay, I'll just wash my face and hands until my clothes get here." She looked into each of the rooms and chose the larger of the two. "How do you know my clothes are in my car?"

He chuckled. "Angel from the motel cafe dates Jason Robard's brother. You met Jason this morning, he's one of the police officers. He texted me a while ago and said you'd checked out of the motel. Not many secrets in town except who the drug supplier is."

Nodding she looked at his face, noticing his posture was stiff, his demeanor while not unfriendly, was not totally open either. She had herself to blame for that, she'd started this morning off rather harshly.

"That's why I like living in a big city."

"Hmm, well, I like knowing who my neighbors are. When I walk into the Copper Cup, I like knowing more than half of the customers in there. I like having my friends close, because honestly, this town is small enough that it's impossible to be all that far, even across town."

He nodded then turned and walked down the steps, his pace a bit quicker than it had been bringing her up. As hurt as she'd been when he didn't call her, she admitted, at least to herself, that things do work out the way they are supposed to; and at that time in her life, she wanted to experience the military and learn all she could learn. She had had thoughts of joining the DEA. Which had meant college and eventually moving anywhere she wanted. That was a curious thing to think about now, after all those years of being pissed at him.

She heard Rory's phone ring downstairs and stepped to the edge of the top step.

"Captain, what do you have?"

## 9

Pulling items from his refrigerator, he berated himself for not going to the grocery store. Not that he'd had the chance lately, but still, even on the way home one night he could have made the effort. Remembering that Odie, a friend from high school, had started his own delivery business, he snagged his phone off the counter. Looking up the webpage on the internet, Odie Eats, he tapped the contact us icon and held his phone to his ear.

"Odie Eats, you've got Odie here."

Chuckling, he said, "Odie, it's Rory Richards, how on earth are you?"

"Rory, my man, I'm fantastic. Business is booming. Who knew there were so many people who didn't want to go out and get things?"

"Well, that's why I'm calling. I haven't had a spare minute in weeks, and I need groceries. How does this work?"

"Check out my website. Click on the store, then the items you want. Pay with your credit card or a payment app, then I'll get a notification. Currently you're looking at about forty-five minutes."

"Perfect. I'm on it. See you then and congratulations on the new business, looks like a winner."

Odie's chuckling could be heard as he ended the call and he couldn't help but smile. Tapping on Odie's website, he found the local grocery store and ordered a variety of items he could use to make a few meals. Next order of business was to get Red's car here. Sending out a text to Jerry, he asked him to swing by and grab her keys, then go back to the station to get her car. If he were out on patrol, that wouldn't be an issue. Someone could follow him and take him back after.

"What's going on?"

Red stood before him, still in her slacks and blouse, but she looked refreshed somehow. He remembered her from the military, she was Army, he was Marine, but they were on base together in Iraq and he noticed her right away. That red hair, her confidence, her ability to adapt to whatever situation they were in. They'd draw fire, have to hunker down and fire back, chase the enemy away and as soon as the mission was over, there'd be a grin on her lips and she'd get to work on cleaning up whatever had to be cleaned up. She never complained. She never shrank back. She never quit. When they got back to the states, they were stationed together for six months. It took him four months to ask her out on an actual date - they went bowling at the arcade on base. But they laughed and gave each other shit all night. It was exhilarating. She was exhilarating. So different from the other women he'd known but that's also what scared the shit out of him. When she got her orders to ship out to Arizona, she squared her shoulders and left without whining, at least that's what it looked like.

He'd said they'd stay in touch. He told her he'd call, but he didn't. Was it a mistake? Probably the biggest of his life. And to see now that it affected her stymied him to no end. He thought she just left as quickly as she'd come without looking back. This thought alone could blow him over with a light breeze.

"Ace?"

Pulling himself from his musings, he cleared his throat, "The Captain said we're to stay here and he spoke to your SAC who's agreed to the plan. He'll send backup if the Captain thinks we need it. The Captain will have everything uploaded into the system soon. Then, we're to look at the video from the convenience mart and the apartment complex and see if you see anyone who looks familiar, suspicious or both. We'll also be able to go over the evidence, though there's very little of it from what he's told me. Tomorrow, we're to call in first thing and see what he wants us to do."

Crossing her arms in front of her, she quipped, "I don't like being locked up like I'm fragile."

"Red, no one thinks you're fragile. He just wants to see if the person who called you makes any kind of move."

His phone chimed that someone breached the security at the end of the street. He walked to the laundry room, which was located next to the garage entry door, and his phone buzzed. Looking out the window he saw Ford's truck pulling up the drive.

Stepping back out to the kitchen, he caught Red's attention. "Ford's here to shore up my security system."

Walking to the garage entry door he tapped on the opener on the wall and opened the garage door for Ford, who climbed from his truck looking a little worse for wear and walked toward him.

"Tough mission?"

"You could say that."

"Come on in and try not to talk our ears off while you're here," he grinned when he said it and got a grunt in response.

Walking into the kitchen, Ford behind him, he watched Red look up from her phone, a hint of a smile on her face, then her eyes rounded when she saw Ford. Ford was what his wife, Debra, had called dark and broody.

"Red, this is Ford Montgomery. Ford, Alice Tucker, DEA."

"Nice to meet you, Alice."

She nodded, smiled and replied, "Nice meeting you."

Rory's phone chimed again, "Ford, I think you remember where everything is. Holler if you need anything in the meantime. Jerry's here to get Red's keys."

She nodded and walked to the staircase and he couldn't not watch her walk away. She had what you'd call a "yoga ass". Perfectly shaped and firm from exercise, likely yoga, but could be anything.

Ford chuckled then turned and walked to the office, which was just off the kitchen and facing the front yard. Scowling slightly, he turned and walked to the garage to wave Jerry in.

Waiting at the entry door for Jerry, he noted the officer exiting his cruiser, and walking toward him with a bit of a stoop. He was dragging, too.

"She's getting her keys, come on in," he called to Jerry, who merely nodded and followed him inside.

Red came down the stairs, keys jingling in her hand and bestowed a glorious smile on Jerry, who then stood taller and graced her with a large smile of his own. To say it didn't irk him would be a lie. It did. A lot.

"Thank you for handling this, Jerry, I appreciate it."

"You got it." Jerry nodded. He half-saluted, turned and walked out the door. Fucker.

Red's phone chimed and he watched her facial expressions as she read the message in her text. Her nose scrunched then relaxed before she tapped a few times, then held the phone to her ear. A moment later she said, "Who died?"

## 10

"It appears they're targeting not only my informant, but his family as well. His brother was found dead about an hour ago. No word on whether he was informing for anyone else, but they're checking." She calmly stated.

"Is that your District?"

She watched Rory's face; he would make a great poker player.

"Yes. He was found in the back-parking lot of a pizzeria in Indianapolis."

"Did you know the brother?"

She briefly bit her bottom lip, then shook her head, "No."

His chest expanded then released as his eyes locked on hers. Ford walked out of the office, looked at Rory and said, "You should call Jared."

He turned then and opened a door next to the office door and descended the basement steps without another word.

Turning her head to watch Rory's reaction as he turned to open the fridge.

"You want a beer?"

"Yes."

Pulling two beers from the fridge he set them on the countertop, twisted the tops off with his hands, which she still admired. His hands were strong, his fingers graceful in a manly way. She'd always enjoyed watching him on his computer or cleaning his gun in service. Sure, strong, flexible, he was coordinated in ways she felt clumsy.

Curiosity was killing her. "Whose Jared?"

He picked up a bottle of beer in each hand, handed her one of them, then tapped his bottle to hers.

"A friend."

She took a long drink and tried not to think about how she'd like to down the whole bottle. She'd never had a drinking problem, but once in a great while, she liked getting lost in absolutely nothing. Having a few drinks and not having to think about death, drugs, destruction, not always in that order.

"Why would you call this friend?"

"Red, how about we sit in the living room and chill? I've got groceries on the way. Jerry will have your car and suitcase here soon. Ford is making sure security is good and we can't go anywhere for a while, so can we just sit?"

She lifted a shoulder in a shrug, turned and walked the few steps into the open concept living room. Sitting on the sofa, which was across the room from the large wall of windows, she allowed her eyes to look out onto the landscape of the backyard. A tall wrought iron fence could be seen across the yard, though it was camouflaged with trees and shrubs in most places.

"How far does the fence go?"

Rory had followed her into the room, sat in the large brown leather recliner and lifted the footrest.

"Around the six houses on this street."

"I didn't see gates when we drove in."

"No gates. We each have security and when the plane is broken at the street entrance, we each get a notification. At first, I wasn't a fan because who wants their neighbors knowing when you come and go? But, over time I've come to like it, we all do, and we watch who's on our street. Plus, times are logged and cars coming and going are recorded so we know when there are deliveries, etc. In other words, we don't have porch pirates."

Taking another long pull from her beer bottle she let that all sink in. Rory did the same.

"Why would you call Jared?"

Rory rubbed his forehead with his fingers, then ran his fingers through his thick dark hair and to his nape. She envied those fingers right now. She loved his hair. How it felt between her fingers, how it smelled, how it looked.

"Jared has special skills on the computer and can find things out our systems can't. Let's just say he colors outside of the lines; we have to stay firmly within ours."

The sound of a metal box closing could be heard, and soon after Ford's footsteps on the stairs echoed. At the top of the steps, Ford looked into the living room at Rory, his eyes flicked to hers, then her beer bottle. A slight grin formed on his face and he didn't look so broody. Actually, he was rather handsome in a dark sort of way.

His voice was deep, and he spoke with a slow deliberate intention.

"You need an upgrade and I've saved the files from the front gates, then cleaned the cache. I can upgrade remotely, which I'll do as soon as I get home. It won't affect anything, and I'll call you after the upgrade is finished so you can reboot the system. Otherwise, all of your security points are operating,"

Rory stood and shook Ford's hand. "Thanks man. How's life these days?"

"Good, great actually. The job is good. Megan is fantastic and Shelby is growing and happy. What more could a man want?"

Rory's smile was outstanding. It hit her hard as she remembered when he used to smile at her like that. She'd sought it out it was so fantastic and now, it was like a punch in the gut how much she'd missed it. Dammit, why did she have to be thrown together with him after all these years and all those tears getting over him? She'd been doing fine. She'd moved on. Excelled even.

His dark handsome head turned toward her, his smile still in place when he said, "Ford has a gorgeous wife and the most beautiful little girl you've ever seen."

And there was Ford's smile again. He reached for his back pocket and pulled out his phone. As if magnetized she stood and walked toward them just as he turned his phone, the picture of a beautiful auburn-haired woman with the prettiest green eyes she'd ever seen holding a dark-haired little girl about ten months old. Megan and Shelby.

"You have a beautiful family, Ford. You're luckier than most I'd say." She meant what she said, but somewhere deep inside it hurt. A child was something she'd always wanted but had never gotten around to having. Life just didn't seem to be lining things up for her to have the sought-after family unit.

"Thank you. I think I'm incredibly blessed. Which also

means, I'm anxious to get back home." He looked again at Rory, "You good here?"

"Yeah." Rory's voice sounded a bit sad, and she couldn't help but wonder if he'd ever wanted a family himself.

Rory's phone chimed and she now recognized that as a signal that someone had turned onto the street. Ford turned but said, "Nice to meet you, Alice."

"Nice meeting you too, Ford."

Rory's phone buzzed this time and she recognized that someone had now pulled into the driveway.

Rory and Ford walked to the garage entrance and she sat on the sofa, suddenly feeling depleted and sad. "Well fuck me, this day continues to deteriorate with every minute." She muttered to herself.

## 11

He watched as Jerry rolled to a stop in front of the far garage door and another car, likely Red's pulled in right behind him. Walking to the garage door panel next to his entry door, he tapped the button for the middle door and ushered the man driving the second car inside. He'd keep Red's car in the garage for protection. Dax climbed out of his cruiser and walked to him. The officer in Red's car exited and walked to him, keys in hand.

Reaching out to hand him Red's keys, he nodded, "Officer Paul Delhurst."

"You're the new guy I've been hearing about."

"Yes, sir. I've actually been on staff for six months now, but since I'm the last hire, I'm the new guy until someone else comes on board."

Jerry stepped up to them, "He's largely working pms, but we're all now usually working doubles."

"Welcome aboard Officer, I'm sorry I haven't met you before now."

"Thank you, sir."

Jerry tapped Paul on the arm, "Let's get cooking, we've got stuff to do before end of shift. Take care, Rory."

"Thanks for the help guys. Keep your heads down and stay safe."

The two officers climbed in Jerry's cruiser and Rory tapped the buttons to close both garage doors. Entering the house, he locked the entry door then sighed. Maybe he'd even get a nap in since they had to be locked down.

Red met him in the hallway to the garage.

"I'd like to get my overnight bag out of my car."

Holding up her keys, he allowed his fingers to graze hers as they exchanged them. He saw that it affected her, her pupils dilated, and she swallowed. When she walked past him, she brushed against him and his brain couldn't get past the fact that she'd done that on purpose. There was plenty of room here, and now his cock was thickening, his heartbeat raced, and her scent still hung in the air. He needed another beer.

Walking to the refrigerator he pulled a bottle from the shelf, turned and saw her empty bottle on the counter and pulled out another one for Red. Setting them both on the counter, he twisted the caps off, slid open the garbage bins, tossed the tops in the garbage and the empty bottles in the back bin. Slowly closing the door, he inhaled a deep breath and closed his eyes trying to remember Debra. All that came to his mind was shiny red hair and crisp green eyes. His heart raced. How could that be? How could he not be able to picture Debra?

"Thanks for taking care of getting my car and my things here, Ace."

Red turned the corner, her overnight bag in her hand. She froze as she looked at him, her head cocked to the right, her brows furrowed.

"Are you alright?"

Sliding a beer bottle across the counter toward her, he nodded once.

"Yeah, Red, I'm fine."

Picking up his bottle he took a long pull of his beer, then walked toward the living room when his phone chimed again.

Stopping halfway there, he turned and said, "Groceries."

He kept walking through the living room and to the front door, looking first out the side windows before opening the door to see Odie walking up the sidewalk with four grocery bags in his arms.

"Odie, thank you so much."

He met him halfway, snagging two bags and walking back to the house. Odie followed him to the kitchen, and he noticed Red was nowhere in sight. Likely upstairs freshening up. That conjured all sorts of naughty thoughts in his mind and his body responded. Shit.

"Thanks for your business, Rory, and thanks for the tip. I'd stay and visit but I've got four more deliveries before I head back for more."

He reached out his hand and Rory shook it, firmly, as he always had, rather sad that he couldn't visit with Odie after all this time, but happy that he had some time to himself to straighten out his thoughts about Red. Closing the door behind Odie, he twisted the deadbolt and reset the alarm. Then he heard the shower running upstairs and muttered under his breath as he walked back to the kitchen. His phone buzzed in his pocket, and he read a text from Ford, short and to the point.

"Reboot."

Changing his direction, he walked to the office and

woke up his laptop. Before rebooting, he opened his photos, searching for older photos of when Debra was alive. Finding an album labeled, Santa Fe he clicked it open to see pictures of their vacation to Santa Fe some ten or more years ago. There she was, her face shiny and bright, a big sombrero on her head, but her smile lit up the whole picture. He stared at her face, guilt crawling up his body because he'd failed to recall her in his mind earlier, his eyes watered slightly, and the shower shut off upstairs.

Shaking the melancholy from his head, he closed the photo album, then rebooted his computer. Time to get back to work; he had a lunch to make, and then they had work to do pouring over the crime scene videos and evidence. No rest for the weary, or was that wicked? Either seemed to work at this juncture.

Unpacking the groceries, he decided on making grilled double ham and cheese sandwiches and a salad. It was one of his favorite lunches.

Gathering the items he needed, he pulled a frying pan from the bottom cabinet and set it on the stove. Pulling a loaf of bread from a grocery bag, he set it on the counter next to the stove, then pulled out the other groceries and finished putting them away. A blow-dryer sounded upstairs and he shook his head to keep thoughts of naked Red out of it.

Slicing the cheddar cheese into medium slices, he lay a piece of cheese on a slice of buttered bread, then stacked the ham on the cheese, then added another slice of cheese, topping it off with a slice of buttered bread. Laying it in the frying pan, he turned the heat down low and put the lid on the pan. Beginning on the second sandwich he heard Red's light footsteps descend the steps and his heartbeat kicked up. He was acting the fool today with all of these ridiculous feelings for a woman he'd left behind years ago. Must be time to get laid again, but that would have to wait until Red was gone.

"It smells fantastic in here."

"Double ham and cheese sandwiches. There's more beer in the fridge if you need one and lunch will be ready in about fifteen minutes."

Walking to the stove he glanced at Red who stood at the counter, a pair of loose-fitting comfortable pants on, like pajamas and a soft looking flowing gray t-shirt. The bra she wore was definitely not padded and didn't need to be as she'd always been well enough endowed that she turned heads. But right now, her nipples strained through the flimsy material she wore, and it was fucking distracting. On top of that, she had a light gloss on her lips and her fresh clean scent wafted across the counter to him and his dick began noticing.

His eyes locked on hers and she smiled, a perfect, beguiling smile.

"Red?"

"What?"

Inhaling deeply, he let out a breath, gritted his teeth and lifted the lid on the pan. Pulling a spatula from the drawer he slid it under the sandwich, flipped it over and added the second sandwich to the pan.

He could sense her walking toward him. The tiny hairs stood on his arms, his lungs struggled to fill with air and his mind was going south faster than a freight train.

He turned when she leaned against the counter, her arms crossed just under her breasts, her left hip jutted out to touch the counter, oh he remembered those hips.

"You can't...what are you trying to do here?"

## 12

"While I was showering, I thought we might as well enjoy ourselves. And, as I remember, something we were very, very good at was enjoying ourselves."

"Aren't you married?"

"No."

"I thought you said you were married for four years."

"I was. I've now been divorced for more than ten years."

She'd missed him. She tried fighting it. Being angry with him earlier sure helped her not remember the things she loved about him, but then she got into the shower and realized a few things. He was going out of his way to make her comfortable. He was down here making them lunch. He was still so friggin' handsome. He still smelled fantastic and when she watched his hands earlier today, she missed them. On her. All over her.

Cooling the water down in the shower did nothing to change the direction of her thoughts and since they were here and both unattached, why didn't they just have some fun?

"Oh. Why didn't you say that?"

"I just did."

"You know what I mean."

"You didn't ask."

"Fuck." He muttered softly under his breath.

He moved away from her to the stove and pulled a delicious smelling sandwich out of the frying pan and lay it on a plate. Quickly flipping the other one, he set the lid back on the pan and cut the first sandwich in two. Walking toward her with the plate he set it in front of her, looked into her eyes like it was the first time. And she looked into his. They said so much about him. She could see who he was by looking deeply into his eyes, he wanted her. He was a man who lived an orderly life, by the looks of his house, which was spic and span. She could see him wrestling with what to do so she made the decision and lifted up on her toes and planted her lips against his.

Her tongue slipped out and slowly swiped along the seam of his lips, the taste of beer still on them. She palmed his face with her right hand, tilting his head slightly so their lips fit perfectly together. She felt his resolve, then she felt it explode as his strong arms wrapped around her body and pulled her tightly to the wall of chest she'd been admiring earlier today. She instantly wrapped her arms around his neck and lifted her legs to wrap them around his waist, which earned her a shove against the counter where she instantly felt his hardness push against her in the most delicious way. She groaned into his mouth and he reciprocated which made her nipples pebble so tightly they tingled.

He moved them down the counter, her ass against the

edge, then he broke their kiss, leaned over and turned off the burner, moved the pan off the hot spot then his hand grabbed her ass, tightly, he squeezed hard and she moaned. He still liked it a bit rough. Perfect.

Kissing along his jaw to his ear, she latched on to his earlobe and nipped at it just hard enough to show him she still liked it that way, too. His large intake of breath excited her beyond reason and his second hand cupped her ass and both hands squeezed tightly.

"Give me what you've got, Ace."

"Fuck." He growled.

One of his hands reached up to the waistband of her lounge pants and pulled it down over her ass exposing her skin to the roughness of his hand. He grabbed her cheek with that hand as the other mimicked the motion, pulling her pants the remainder of the way down her ass. His eager fingers didn't stop long, and he reached around as far as he could and explored her naked flesh, moving roughly past her asshole and further up, almost but not quite where she wanted him to be. Arching her back to give him more access the tip of his finger slipped inside of her and she whimpered.

"More." She groaned into his ear.

Before her head could register what was happening, he set her feet on the ground, spun her around, grabbed her pants and tugged, then quickly undid his pants. Soon he pushed gently on her shoulders to bend her over the counter and the tip of his cock was at her entrance.

"You sure?"

"God, yes."

He thrust inside of her with a force that made her want more so that's what she asked for.

"More, Ace. Harder."

He obliged. Shoving himself into her again and again, with the strength she'd remembered, maybe more now that they were both grown. She shoved back as far as she could to take him all the way inside of her. She faintly realized she'd likely have bruises on her ribs, but she didn't give a shit as she held her right hand up to brace herself against the wall so she could feel him completely, he then pulled her back a bit and his delightful fingers found her clit and quickly circled, adding pressure after every couple of circles.

Her breathing increased and her vision, well that was gone. Her heartbeat raced, the feel of his cock sliding in her, the best feeling in the world, the memories of the past now replaced with this one, which she would remember forever.

"My God, Ace. Shit." She panted.

He increased his speed, their pace rapid and wild and she loved it.

"Ohmigod. Ohmigod." Her orgasm hit like a flood wall and he pulled out and growled as she felt the warm sticky ropes of cum shoot onto her ass.

His breathing was ragged but he managed to huff out, "Fuck that's hot." And she knew he was watching himself cum on her. She lay her head on the cool granite of the countertop and allowed herself a moment to lock this memory away and catch her breath, in that order.

## 13

He finished cleaning himself up, changed his boxer briefs and his Khakis then walked out of his bedroom to the living room. Red was still upstairs, and his eyes floated to the second level where he could hear the water running. Taking in a deep breath his mind whirled at the speed at which things had happened today and he was trying to keep up. They'd always had amazing chemistry, even before he'd screwed up the nerve to ask her out.

Continuing to the kitchen, he slid the frying pan to the burner on the stove and turned the burner on to once again heat up their sandwiches. His thoughts floated to Red, back when they dated so darned many years ago, what was it 15 or more years? How was it she was as sexy as ever and felt better than he remembered? So much about her dug into him and he could feel her taking hold. He had to stop that. As soon as they stopped this drug operation, they'd be once again facing her leaving and either not seeing each other again or a long-distance relationship. History had a way of repeating itself.

Letting out a long breath as warm hands circled his waist from behind and slid sensuously up his abdomen. Her breasts pressed against his back, then her head lay against the back of his shoulder where she sighed.

"That felt amazing, Ace."

Slowly he turned in her arms, moving them away from the stove. Her head then rested against his shoulder and he lay his head on top of hers as he encircled her in his arms.

"You felt amazing, Red."

Her phone rang out the song Close to My Enemies. Her head popped off his chest, her brows furrowed.

"That's Sergio's ringtone."

"So, someone has his phone. But when they called you earlier today, didn't they used a different phone?"

"Yes."

"Hmm, let's be smart about this and find out what game they're playing."

She snagged her phone from the counter where she'd left it, looked at the readout, turned the phone to him and he saw the name Twitch. She mouthed Sergio and he nodded.

Taking a deep breath, she tapped the green answer icon and quickly tapped the speaker icon.

"Who am I speaking with?"

"Well now, Hightop, who do you think it is?"

"I'm not in the mood to play games. What do you want?"

Her green eyes narrowed, and her lips tightened. Scared or mad she could look fierce. Her quick temper rose but he knew it would dissipate just as fast.

Laughter from the other end of the phone could be

heard. Quickly pulling his phone from his back pocket, he tapped the record icon and lay his phone on the counter. Red's eyes met his and held.

"I just wanted to see how you were doing since you saw what a great job I did on Sergio or what is it you called him? Twitch?"

"If you don't have anything productive to say, I'm ending this call right now."

More laughter and his temper started to rise. This asshole wanted to play cat and mouse with her.

"I simply wanted to offer you an invitation."

"An invitation to what?"

"I thought you and me should have a sit down. Since I know you were paying Twitch, I thought maybe you'd like to pay me something to go away."

"Huh, you think the Indiana State Police will pay you to go away from Indiana? Then what, you'll set up shop in a different state? Or come back in a few years and do it again?"

"Look, Hightop, I think we can make a great deal here. You get what you want, we move our operation out of the state, and I get paid to move said operation. It seems like we both win."

He shook his head no. She was not going to meet with this asshole. She would not make a deal with them. They didn't buy off criminals to make their problems go away, they put them in jail where they ceased all drug operations.

She looked away from him and his heart began a rapid cadence.

"Where do you propose this meeting take place?"

No. No. No.

He wrapped his hand around her right upper arm to get her attention, but she shrugged him away.

"Glad to see you might be interested. I'll call you in one hour to discuss this further."

The line went dead and she grabbed her phone and ended the call. He stopped the recording on his phone, both angry and bewildered at the lengths she would go to get this operation off the streets.

"Red, you cannot be thinking about meeting with him? It'll be a set up and you could end up dead."

"I'm going to explore all of my options, Ace. I've been working on this case for more than two years. I'm getting close. Last night told me that. This morning confirmed it. They know I'm getting close too or they wouldn't have gone to such lengths. And to offer to move out for money, that's a new one. They must be getting nervous."

She tapped a few times on her phone then held it to her ear. "Plus, I'm up for promotion next month, I want it."

She tapped her phone a couple of times put it to her ear then waited, "Ben, they've made contact and want to meet to discuss me paying them off to move from Indiana."

His guts twisted; she could not be considering this.

Moving back to the stove and flipping the sandwiches into the hot frying pan he braced himself for the inevitable. Then it dawned on him, this is what bothered him about her all those years ago. Her confidence scared the shit out of him because it was easy to be too confident. Being too confident got people killed.

His eyes glazed as he watched the cheese on their sandwiches begin to drip down the bread and onto the hot pan, then bubble and brown. Flipping each sandwich over, the aroma of his favorite sandwich wafted in the puffs of steam that rose from the pan. His stomach growled then tightened as he heard Red end her call with, "I'll wait for your call."

---

## 14

She was close, so close. Once she finally brought down this drug syndicate, she'd get that promotion. Then she could have her pick of other jobs, either within the DEA or FBI, where she'd be an FBI Special Agent until the age of 57. She could really set down some roots. That's all she really wanted. All her years in the service she'd moved from base to base. Then she left the Army and went to college so she could join the DEA. After her training in the DEA, she was transferred as Special Agent to a few different Divisions over the years. Once she'd gotten her position in the Chicago IL DEA Division and was assigned to the Indianapolis District Office, she thought she'd finally have a place to call home base. But in the three years she'd been in Indy, she'd been on one assignment or another, either with her District's teams or on her own helping law enforcement agencies more than she'd been at the District Office. She knew this would be her life when she joined the DEA, but she was growing tired of it all.

Looking around here at Rory's home she felt cheated

of this. A home. A dog. Maybe a couple of babies. She was still young enough to have them, though at 37, she was nearing the end of her career fighting drug cartels, suppliers, syndicates. DEA Special Agents couldn't be older than 37, so it was earn this promotion for the job she wanted or be transferred to some other location and feel like a newbie again and be located who knew where. And time for bearing children was ticking away.

"Red?"

Glancing up at Rory, he held two plates with the most delicious looking sandwiches on them. He nodded to the table and she tried to smile, but her brain was already working on possible scenarios.

Sitting at the table, in front of one of the sandwiches, Rory walked to the refrigerator and pulled two more beers from the bottom shelf. Twisting the tops on each of them, he tossed the caps in the garbage, then came and sat at a right angle to her. Handing her a bottle he nodded, but he didn't smile, and her stomach tightened. He was mad.

"Smells good, Ace. I didn't know you cooked."

"I love cooking. I haven't had the time to cook lately, and this is nothing compared to some of the meals I've learned to make, but it's pretty fucking good."

She picked up one half of the sandwich and bit into it. She hadn't had breakfast and the morning had been a bit of a blur, but her stomach appreciated her eating now and it was fantastic.

"Omigod." She tried talking with her mouth full of sandwich and choose to wait until she finished so she didn't make a pig of herself.

Swallowing and taking a swig of beer, she continued, "Ace, this is wonderful."

"Thanks." He bit into his sandwich and looked out the sliding doors on to the backyard.

Taking his lead, she quietly ate her sandwich trying to puzzle out what she had that was getting her near enough to scare this operation out in the open.

"Do you want to talk about it?"

She looked into his eyes and realized he was allowing her to piece things together out loud.

"I do." She finished half of her sandwich, then took another drink of beer.

"Twitch has been informing for me for about five years. At first it was petty stuff. Then it became bigger stuff. His reasons were his own, but what I deduced was that his nephew got hooked pretty bad on drugs and OD'd. It made him realize what he'd been doing, and he started turning on the people who supplied him. We brought down a couple of low-level pushers. A few street thugs and dealers and an enforcer for one of the suppliers. Then, something changed, I don't know what. Twitch started telling me about "The Big Guy". He'd disappear for a while and then come back with information. I asked him once if he was going in deeper to get me information and he only said, "Worth it.""

Wiping her fingers on the white paper napkin alongside her plate, she changed her position on her chair, folding her left leg under her right and twisting slightly to face him.

"Then, last week he told me about the deal going down last night. I think what you saw was simply a low-level street dealer who'd just gotten a large load to distribute. I do think it's happening in one of those apartments next to the convenience store where you had parked. It's too much of a coincidence that I'd be told to go to the apartment complex to see the big drop and then that Twitch would be found dead outside of the Longstone Apartment building, only for "The Big Guy" or whoever to see us leave this morning. So, I'm thinking there's a vantage point in one of those upper apartments that they use, probably in Longstone given its location. They must be able to see a point of interest or have some reason that they've chosen that place. And, it seems unlikely that a high-level trafficker would hole up in a shitty apartment building unless it is very profitable. So, it appears that's the place I've been looking for."

Rory twisted to face her head on and leaned forward on the table. "Why here? What is it about Lynyrd Station? They could blend in easier in a larger city."

"Right, but what do you have here that is more attractive than blending in?"

"Off the top of my head, I'm thinking a supply system. After Limitless was taken down by the cops and Victor Santarino was killed, Mangus went into hiding, but continued the family's illegal activities. Mangus was moving and smuggling some things, including arms and jewels, underground through tunnels near his hideout at the bottom of Ryker Mountain. Mangus' minions dug tunnels through the mountain so they could move without being seen. There was always a suspicion that the Santarinos were moving drugs as well as arms and jewels."

"Okay, who has access to those tunnels now?"

"There was a huge shootout that brought down Mangus and his gang. It's a result of the shootout mostly that the family and former minions, whose pictures I showed you, are dead or in prison. Dodge Sager, who's a friend of Ford's and mine, took Mangus down. I'll have to check, but not till all the law enforcement agencies are finished with their investigations, since the property on Ryker Mountain is owned by the Santarinos or one of their companies, and the family must still have access to it. But, any of them that were in the United States are either dead or in prison."

Leaning back, she pushed her hands through her hair and into a ponytail at her crown. Rory's eyes floated to her arms, then down to her chest, then back up to her eyes. It made her feel sexy. Alive. Wanted. Gawd she'd missed feeling like that. She'd folded herself up into her career these past few years and made work her life. Had she been stupid all these years? When she looked at how Rory had made a home and tried living a normal life, she realized how she'd fallen so short at making any kind of life for herself.

"We should check with Immigration and Homeland Security to see if they have travel records of any members of the Santarino family. You should check with DEA since we know that some of their activity internationally was drug trafficking."

He pulled his phone from his pants pocket and tapped a couple of times.

"Captain, can we have someone check with Immigration and Homeland Security to see if the Santarinos or anyone associated with them traveled to the US in the past year?"

## 15

B eautiful. Smart. Sexy. Badass. All rolled up in a creamy-skinned, redhead who made his heart race. Why did life have to keep putting them in proximity with each other only to pull them apart? His life was here. This was his home. His parents were here. Debra was buried here. His siblings were here. Most of all, he loved it here. He had a gorgeous home, friends, a fantastic job. He had it all. Except her.

Picking up their empty dishes he loaded them in the dishwasher, wiped down the counter, walked to the laundry room and tossed the dishrag in the washer, then came back to the kitchen. Red had gotten up and walked to the living room. Her silhouette shown in the large floor to ceiling windows looking out on to the backyard, the light created shadows. The shadow of her form wholly appealing. Inhaling deeply, he walked into the living room as his phone rang.

"Richards." He snapped, surprised at his own terseness.

"None of the Santarinos are here in the States. The

daughter, Francesca is out of prison and back in Italy. Rumor has it she's learning the ropes from grandpa, but that's none of our business now; Italian authorities need to deal with their own shit."

"Thanks, Captain. Who is controlling Mangus' hideout on Ryker Mountain and any other buildings and land here in the States that the Santarinos or their companies own? The building Limitless is in, the home on the mountain Victor used, and especially all those tunnels they dug "

He could hear his Captain clicking on his keyboard, while his own eyes were glued to Red. She turned to stare at him, just as eager for information as he was.

"The Limitless International building and land is for sale, sitting empty now and listed with a realtor in town, Van Steel Realty. It's been empty since authorities shut the place down."

He sat in his recliner, elbows on his knees. "Does anyone go in periodically and check to make sure no one is using the place for illegal operations?"

He heard his Captain take a deep breath. "We don't have authority. We could see if the realtor minds letting us in, but she doesn't have to."

Red nodded her head and he agreed with her. "I think it's worth a shot, Captain. Maybe that's something Tucker and I could do. I know Margery Van Steel from my shooting pool days. Maybe she'd do me a solid."

"I don't see that that could do any harm. But, try not to get in trouble. I'll send Officer Delhurst to back you up in case there's trouble. Let me know when you've made contact and keep me posted on what you find. Also, evidence has been uploaded, so you two need to look it over and write up a report."

The line went dead before he could say anything more. They were short staffed at the department and having him and Red off the beat for a while sure didn't help. Maybe they'd get lucky and find something at Limitless.

"Evidence is uploaded, Red. I'll log you in on to my computer while I call Maggie and see if we can get her to let us in Limitless."

"What if she doesn't let us in?"

He stood, suddenly weary beyond reason. "A rock through a window might be enough to let us go and check things out."

Her smile was brilliant. "I love the way you think, Ace. I had you pegged for strait-laced and buttoned-up. Glad to see I was wrong."

"The Santarinos brought a lot of shit to this town and we thought we were finished with them. So doing something outside the lines a bit isn't the worst thing to make sure they truly are shut down for business. Ford has it made with his company. They color outside the lines quite a bit. But they get shit done. But, of course, they're not cops like we are."

"You've mentioned this company before; I'm intrigued beyond reason."

Shaking his head he silently chastised himself. "I can't really discuss it, Red. If he wants to share it, that's his business."

"Fair enough." She shrugged her slender shoulders and walked toward his office. Her scent wafted to him as she passed and goosebumps formed on his arms. He needed to put some distance between them and soon.

He let out a long breath and followed Red into the office. She stood staring at his computer, which was running a slide show of pictures, mostly of Debra and him in their better times. Some of him in the service. Some of his siblings Rochelle, Rourke and Rowan at Christmas. A picture of Debra laughing at him at his mom and dad's anniversary party slid onto the screen and Red's head cocked to the side.

"She looks happy."

"I suppose she was then." He moved to shake his mouse and stop the pictures. She reached out and took his hand before he could do that.

"Were you happy?"

She turned then so they were facing each other, and he saw seriousness in her eyes. He cleared his throat.

"I was at first."

"But not later?"

"No." His voice was quiet, as if saying it out loud made him a bad person.

Her hand cupped his cheek.

"Why?" Now her voice was quiet.

"Red, this is a heavy conversation..."

"Why?"

Inhaling deeply, he let it out slowly and tried to relax.

"At first she was a lot like you. Confident. Strong. Independent. Then she grew needy. She hated my job because it often kept me out late or had me up early. She liked consistency; I couldn't offer that. She grew more and more depressed. I grew more and more irritated, frustrated and pulled in multiple directions. On the day she was killed, we'd had a fight. Afterward, she still was very upset; she'd packed a bag for a few days and was going to stay with her parents for a while. We were never able to work it out because she was killed on her way to their place."

Her arms wrapped around his shoulders and pulled

him to her body as she whispered. "Oh, Ace. I'm so sorry. That's a lot of guilt to hold on to."

Wrapping his arms around her waist, he pulled her close and enjoyed the way her body curved into his. When he held her like this, it felt like they were made for each other. Just like this. Working together. Making love. Talking. Understanding.

As if she read his thoughts, she said, "Not everyone understands people like us."

# 16

He hugged her tightly, his arms strong and solid around her and she never felt more secure. When his head dipped down to rest against hers, so they were temple to temple, the roughness of his whiskers against her cheek sent shivers the length of her body. The gruffness in his voice when he whispered in her ear, "Not many do, but I know you do." Well, that sent a riot of emotions running through her body and mind.

She closed her eyes against the moisture forming in them. The harsh reality was that they once again lived in different places and had careers to tend to. Careers that they'd both worked their entire lives to earn and they were more than a hundred miles apart on the map.

He kissed her temple then and bent over his computer, shaking the mouse to stop the photographs from scrolling past, and quickly logged on to the police database so she could look at evidence. He then sat in a chair across the room, his relaxed posture belying his emotions because she'd felt the slight tremors that ran through his body just now. She felt them, too.

Out of the corner of her eye she watched him pull his cell phone from his pocket, and scroll through what she assumed were phone numbers, then tapped on one and sat back in the chair, crossing his left ankle over his right knee.

"Maggie, it's Rory, how are you?"

He smiled at what this Maggie said in his ear and she pushed down that little green monster that threatened to rise up.

"No, not interested in selling, I just got things the way I like them, think I'll enjoy it for a while."

His chuckle was deep in his chest and genuine, she must be a friend, but hopefully not a former lover.

"No, I understand you're selling the Limitless International building and properties. I wondered if it would be possible to go in and take a look around?"

Scrolling quickly past the pictures of Twitch's carved up face and hunk of tongue lying alongside his body, she'd leave that for the forensic lab, she was mostly interested in anything that led them to one of the apartments.

"How much?" He whistled. "That's rather steep for a tainted building and land."

Dropping his crossed leg, he leaned forward, placed his elbows on his knees, his eyes cast down to the hard-wood floor between his feet.

"Okay, what do you need. I can get the pre-approval this afternoon."

Appearing at the opposite side of the desk, he leaned forward and grabbed a pen laying alongside the computer she worked on. Pulling a post-it note from a wire holder on the desktop, he wrote a string of numbers, then an email address.

"Okay, I'll be in touch in a bit. Take care."

Ending his call, he began dialing another number and she continued to read the evidence with halfhearted interest.

"Captain, I need to get a bank pre-approval for the purchase of the Limitless real estate before we can get in. Put it in Alice Thomas' name."

Her eyes looked across the desktop where his impressive package or at least the zipper of his Khakis was facing her. Frustrated with herself for the thoughts she was thinking and maybe more importantly, the one's she wasn't, she reminded herself she was a grown-ass woman and not a teenager. But, he did have a nice package. One of the best.

"Four million dollars."

She could hear the Captain's voice on the other end of the phone, and he sounded rather stressed. I suppose putting the department on the line for four million dollars was a bit of a stressor, but for some reason, it made her smile.

"I'll wait to hear from you."

He tapped his phone then set it on the desk. "Do you have anything of interest yet?"

Oops, she'd better start paying attention. "Not yet."

Pulling her head together, she dove into the evidence file and began reading the police report, the evidence database, the forensic report, and the Medical Examiner's report. Once she'd finished with that police report, she came across the police reports from last night and looked those over checking the witness statements for similarities. There were four in total, from different residents of the apartment complex. They read the same, shots fired, yelling, drug deals going down in the common area between the buildings, needles, lighters, light bulbs found lying around all the time. The complaints went on and on.

Rory left the room and came back in a few minutes later, set a laptop on the desk, then pulled the chair up to the other side. Opening the top, he began typing, then finally said to her, "I'm in the evidence database. What have you found so far?"

"How many computers do you have here?"

His eyes landed on hers, a slight amount of humor in them, "Why does it matter?"

Shaking her head, she honestly didn't know why. "This house is much more expensive than most cops can afford. You have fantastic furniture. Not one but two computers, one a laptop, state of the art security. What gives, Ace?"

Inhaling deeply, he leaned forward slightly, his voice lowered and took on a gruffness usually only heard when he made love to her.

"You think I'm dirty, Red?"

"No, you've always been too honest for that. But, how can you make it like this?"

It became more important than she cared to admit, and not because of the money, but because of the mystery of the money. If that made sense.

"Red, I don't like talking about this stuff, but so I can ease your beautiful mind, I happen to have a fair amount of money. My grandparents made a good living, very good. Entrepreneurial his whole life, my grandfather started several businesses in his days. When they died, my siblings and I inherited. When Debra died, I inherited again. She was from an incredibly wealthy family, not that it mattered because we never asked for a dime from either side of our families. But I had to lose people in order to become a wealthy man. I try hard not to flaunt it, but the work I do, we do, requires a lot of mental fortitude. When I come home, I want my sanctuary. A place I can unwind, settle in and utilize to equalize my stressors. So, I spent a fair amount of money on this house and setting it up to suit me. And, my car, I spent money on her."

Leaning back in her chair she assessed his eyes, his features, and concluded that he wasn't lying.

"Usually rich boys don't join the military and serve, how many tours, three? How did your family feel about that?"

His right shoulder raised and lowered. "They weren't thrilled with my choice, but they respected it. What they're not happy about now is my job. But we just agree to disagree on that."

Nodding she saw him in a new light. He wasn't spoiled and living on the family trust fund, he was admirable in a whole new way to her. As if that was possible.

His phone rang and he tapped the speaker icon. "Captain, what do you have?"

## 17

H e hated talking about his money. Either people wanted something from you afterward or they treated you differently. Most of his coworkers didn't even know how much money he had. Of course, they knew his grandparents were wealthy, after all it was a small town. But they naturally assumed his parents inherited that money. He'd heard a couple of cops gossiping once about him and he'd shut that down right away.

Now he stood in his kitchen waiting for Red to grab her shoes so they could go over to the Limitless building. He felt restless and a little bit relieved. Which was a surprise to him to feel relieved that Red knew about his money. That was new.

The sound of her running down the steps, a new vigor in them now that they'd been sprung from house arrest. It was horrible feeling trapped. It was also nearing 6:00 p.m. and would be dark soon, not that they were actually looking at the building to purchase, but he wanted Maggie to think so.

"All set, Ace. I feel like I'm being released from prison." Her smile was infectious.

"Me, too." He started for the garage as soon as she'd reached him, and he had to stop himself from reaching out and grabbing her hand. Giving his head a slight shake, he opened the door to the garage and stepped back to allow her to precede him. She did with a smile on her face and damn if it didn't make him feel good.

She climbed into the passenger side of his car and he jumped in the driver's side, tapped the button to open the garage door and started her up. The roar of the V-8 engine always gave him a thrill and he couldn't help the smile that appeared on his face.

"Sexy sound." Red whispered.

He simply nodded his agreement.

"Okay, so Maggie is a friend from back when I shot pool for the Copper Cup. She used to tend bar there until her real estate business took off. She's smart, savvy, and very good at reading people. We need to go in as if we're purchasing for your family. She doesn't know you; she doesn't know your family. So, let's say you're a friend from the service here scoping out the building and I came along with you for fun."

"You think she'll buy that?"

"I don't know. But what she needs to do is relay that information to whoever in the Santarino family has hired her. As to what she really believes, I highly doubt she'll relay any thoughts to them. She just wants to make a commission."

"Okay. That's plausible."

"And, Officer Delhurst will meet us there as a precaution."

"What are you telling Maggie about that?"

He chuckled. "He's your security detail."

She laughed and it was amazing. He glanced over to see her smiling face and it was like the sun shone right into the car. Stunning.

She was quiet for a while and it was pleasant riding and not feeling tension.

"Is Maggie an old girlfriend?"

"Nope."

"Friend with benefits?"

"Nope."

Glancing over at her he saw a slight smile on her face, and he couldn't help the grin on his.

"Were you jealous?"

"Nope."

They both laughed.

"She had a baby around seven months ago. The father is rather mysterious. No one's seen him and rumor has it he's some wealthy businessman from out of town."

"Rumors, sometimes they have a ring of truth to them."

Pulling into the Limitless parking lot, Delhurst's cruiser was already there but he wasn't inside. Red noticed it too as he could see her scanning the outside of the building looking for him. Maggie's car wasn't in the lot yet, so he must have been walking around alone.

Stopping in front of the main door, he put the Charger in Park and undid his seat belt. Delhurst appeared around the East corner of the building to their left and they both relaxed.

"Ready?" he asked, knowing full well she was.

"Let's do this."

Her phone rang then, and she pulled it from the pocket of her jacket, looked at the readout and said, "It's the number from this morning."

"Go ahead and answer it."

"What?" She answered and he at once admired her spunk and worried she was too brash. He also had to remind himself that she'd been doing this for years and she had her methods.

"I've thought about it; but I'm not interested in working on your behalf to ask the State of Indiana to pay you to do anything. You're a criminal and neither Indiana nor the USA negotiates with criminals."

She pulled her phone from her ear and tapped the speaker icon.

"Well you paid Twitch to snitch for you."

"You don't know anything about what I did and didn't do with Twitch."

"I think you need to mind your manners, Hightop. I believe I'm calling the shots here. I can easily cut your tongue out and carve up your face just like Twitch, so watch yourself."

The line went dead and he saw Red take a deep breath. "He's scared about something."

She opened her door and hopped out ready to get to work. He shook his head, unsure of his feelings about her being threatened and her casual attitude concerning it. But then he remembered, this was the Red he'd known except now she also was an experienced DEA Special Agent. She loved the action.

Delhurst stopped on the sidewalk in front of the door, waiting for them to reach him.

"Checking the perimeter, Delhurst?"

Nodding, he replied. "Yes, sir. Just in case there was anything going on."

"See anything?"

"No, sir."

A car pulling into the lot had them all turning to see a gleaming white Cadillac Escalade stopping alongside Rory's car. Maggie popped out of her car, a huge smile on her face, her dark hair shining in the waning streams of sunlight, her over-sized sunglasses reflecting the rays off the little rhinestones on the bows.

Maggie walked to him; her slender form tightly encased in a black pencil skirt with a white blouse tucked into it. A large gold chain hung around her neck and a substantial diamond bracelet glittered on her wrist. She screamed expensive.

"Rory, so good to hear from you and see you. I got the pre-approval for Ms. Thomas a while ago, so we're all set."

She hugged him and he hugged her back, though not like he'd hugged Red earlier, and it sure didn't feel as warm and inviting as Red's hug had felt. Weird.

"Maggie, I'd like you to meet Alice Thomas. She's a friend from the military and her family is interested in moving one of their businesses to Lynyrd Station. I'm along for the ride."

Maggie held out her hand and Red promptly grasped it and shook. By the ever-so-slight grimace on Maggie's face, he believed Red probably made sure the handshake was firm. Showing her dominance at the beginning, that was so Red.

"Okay, well let's start inside. I see you brought police protection."

He responded first. "Yes, Alice's father is rather protective and he's heard about some of our issues here lately; it almost caused him to reconsider this place. But the Mayor has been trying to get someone in this building for a while and talked him into giving us a chance in Lynyrd Station."

"I'm so glad he rethought pulling out. We all know you

are working feverishly to stop the recent flood of crime. It's only a matter of time and it'll be gone."

Using her phone to unlock the lockbox that held the key, Maggie inserted it into the deadbolt on the door; she opened it wide allowing them to precede her then quickly turned on the lights.

The air was surprisingly fresh for an empty, locked up building and he knew Red was thinking the same thing. Her red hair gleamed in the overhead lights, but her eyes were taking in everything. He saw her nose flare and twitch slightly as she was sniffing the air trying to puzzle out a few things that already didn't add up.

"Would you like to see the upstairs first or the main level?" Maggie asked.

Red smiled at her before responding, "I'd like to see the upstairs first if you don't mind."

"Certainly." Maggie walked to the left of the doorway that lead to a staircase. They each walked up quietly, he following Red and Delhurst behind him.

On the second floor Maggie switched the lights on and the pristinely polished dark wood floors gleamed under the lights. Walking to the end of the long hallway, Maggie opened the door, reached in and flipped the switch but stood outside of the office.

"This was the President's office. As you'll see it's beautifully appointed."

The white carpeting muffled the sounds of their footsteps and in its place made a swishing sound as they each entered the room. The mahogany desk was clear except for a telephone, a desk lamp, and a small wooden holder for pens. Everything was neat and tidy and while you could imagine someone loving to have this office, he knew the dirty secrets it held, and to him there was no appeal at all.

A small conference table stood to the right, and a credenza behind the desk held a neatly stacked pile of folders, which seemed out of place in the room.

Officer Delhurst walked to the stack of folders and glanced down but then turned to face them. Red looked around then stepped out of the room, and he and Delhurst followed.

They did the same type of perusal of the other offices on the second floor and he recognized Skye's office from Lincoln's description of it. He could picture her in this room, it wasn't nearly as pretentious as the others, which was Skye Winters. She was gorgeous and would make many models feel lacking, but she wasn't pretentious in the slightest.

Entering the break room, they had seen enough, and descended the stairs to the main level. Since this was the area that was largely an art gallery when the Santarinos were alive, there was a vast open space, gleaming floors and five-star bathrooms but little else.

"Okay, what do you think so far?" Maggie asked.

"It's impressive, but I would like to see the loading docks and shipping areas," Red responded.

Maggie's smile faltered which was unusual, of course a buyer would want to see the whole building. But she caught herself and turned to lead them to the back of the main gallery area and through a door. A short hallway led them to another door which opened to a metal staircase leading down to the shipping area.

Red's back straightened and she stepped down from the bottom step and her eyes scanned the entire area. Delhurst was alert as well, walking slowly around the perimeter of the room. At one point he bent over and picked something up and dropped it in a nearby garbage can and then kept on moving. Looking at each of the dock doors, Red surveyed the area and he rather enjoyed watching her work.

She turned to Maggie and said, "If my father would like to come and take a look at it, will you be available later this week?"

"Of course." Maggie's smile returned and she promptly pulled a spec sheet and a business card from the folio she carried and handed the information to Red. "I'll email you the other specs I have on the building just let me know if you're interested. My email is on the card and, of course, Rory knows how to reach me as well."

Red smiled, but it didn't reach her eyes. "Yes, of course, Rory knows how to reach you."

## 18

Rory's door chimed as he got in his car and waited as she hesitated and glanced around as if surveying the area. What she was really doing was watching Maggie out of the corner of her eye. The look Maggie leveled on Delhurst sent a chill through her, something was up. She climbed into the passenger seat, buckled her seat belt, and asked, "How well do you know her? And, no I'm not jealous, but there's something off about her and I can't put my finger on it."

He started the car and put it in reverse, easing out of the parking space before Maggie. "I don't know her all that well, I suppose. As I told you, she was a bartender while I shot pool and I knew she was also working real estate. She's called me a few times over the past couple of years to see if I was interested in selling my house, but nothing more than that. And, I mentioned her baby daddy is a mystery as well."

"Do you know anyone who knows her better?"

He navigated the car out of the parking lot, his eyes scanning the darkening road in the diminishing sunlight.

"I can make some inquiries. What specifically are you looking for, personal information or business as in her real estate sales history?"

"Personal."

He wasn't looking at this like an outsider and that had been his mistake all along; he knew these people too well and trusted them, at least as much as a cop can. In that way, she had the advantage.

"Let me think on who I can call."

She nodded. "What about this Jared that Ford mentioned."

"Red, you want to color outside the lines?"

"Sometimes we have to be inventive. Is it really coloring outside the lines to gather information? I just want something that can lead me in a legal direction to search. Is she selling so much real estate that she can afford the Cadillac, diamond bracelet, thick gold chain and have her nails and hair done regularly?"

"But, if we do have to go to court or prove our trail is legit, we have to account for how we got the intel."

"Maybe. It sounds like you don't want me digging into your 'friend's' life. Care to share?" The edge to her voice took on a different tone and she reminded herself not to let this get personal. Sure, Maggie was gorgeous and everything she wasn't. Sophisticated. Womanly. A smart dresser.

His voice broke into her self-defeating thoughts. "Nope."

He tapped the call icon on his dash and the robotic voice activated, "Please say a command."

"Call Jared Timms."

"Calling Jared Timms."

Jared's phone ringing sounded on the speaker system in the car.

"Yeah."

Rory chuckled, "Hey Jared, it's Rory."

"Dude, I know who it is. What can I do for you?"

"What can you find out about Margery Van Steel? Mostly personal. She has a mysterious baby daddy, and she's driving a brand-new Cadillac Escalade and dripping in jewelry. Is she selling that much real estate or is baby daddy funding her expensive lifestyle?"

"Okay, you know this costs, right?"

"Yep, no worries there."

Jared chuckled on the other end of the phone. "I know, man."

The call ended and the car was silent for a while.

"I take it he knows about your money."

Rory inhaled deeply and let it out slowly. "Red, there's very little Jared doesn't know."

Rory pulled his car into the garage and shut it off.

"I know we had a late lunch, but I'm getting a bit hungry, how about pizza and a couple of beers?"

She sighed, "That sounds fantastic."

It did. For all of Maggie's polish and poise she highly doubted the woman would drink beer and eat pizza. And again, what was it that bugged her so about Maggie? Seriously she needed to get her out of her head.

She followed Rory to the door, and when he opened the door then stood back to let her go in before him, she got goosebumps on her arms. It was thrilling to have a man be solicitous to her. She'd played the tough cookie all of her life and usually men just treated her like one of the guys, which generally, she liked. With Rory, she didn't want to be a guy; she was a woman and damn it all anyway, she was majorly attracted to Rory Richards. Even if her heart would be broken in a few days. Again. Likely forever.

She walked into the kitchen and stopped at the counter as his strong arms wrapped around her from behind.

His deep voice, took on a slight gruffness as he whispered in her ear, "I enjoy watching you work, Red. You're an impressive woman. Beautiful. Strong. Smart. The whole package."

Her nipples pebbled and a warm sensation ran through her body and landed between her legs. The warmth of his body against her back brought back a flood of memories of their afternoon sexcapades and she wanted to feel like that again. Wanted in such a powerful way, he didn't even hesitate to take her.

She pushed her ass back into the hardness she felt burgeoning behind his zipper and was met with his right hand sliding down her body to hold her hip as he pushed harder into her rear end.

"Red." His voice was barely above a whisper and sounded as if he was struggling to keep himself in check. The thought of his losing control with her sent another flood of emotions running through her body. She pushed back again only to have his arms wrap tighter around her body, holding her captive against him. His lips found her ear and his tongue dipped inside just a bit then his teeth nipped the outer edges.

"You want it again Red 'cause I sure do."

"Yes." She could barely get the word out her breathing was so stilted.

He released her and spun her around, his lips capturing hers firmly, before softening and caressing her lips in such a provocative way. Soft, wet lips danced with hers, coaxing her to give him more and more of her. His tongue slid into her mouth, touching each surface, mating with her tongue, his hardness pushing against her hitting that spot that was likely to drive her wild if he kept it up.

"This time, I intend to watch you."

Gawd. Right now she couldn't even form words.

He lifted her and her legs immediately wrapped around his hips as he carried her to the bedroom. Periodically he nipped at her throat, her jaw and her earlobe, just enough to feel but not to cause pain and she wanted more.

He lay her on the bed, his voice now gruff and rugged, just as she liked it. "Take your clothes off while I watch you. On the bed. I want to see you wiggle around."

The dimness of the light in this room lent itself to romance. Small shafts of light filtered in from the living room and a small night light on the wall added a yellowish hue to the room. She could see his features as she unbuttoned her blouse, slowly and he pulled his shirt over his head in a millisecond and let it drop to the floor.

Wriggling out of her blouse, he smiled and undid the button and zipper of his pants, pushing them down his sexy, firm hips and stepping out of them, his eyes never left her body. She arched her back to unfasten her bra and he smiled, though it was Cheshire cat like, he was a man whose prey was performing for him. As soon as her bra loosened, she pulled it off and let it lay on the bed, her hands immediately began unbuttoning her slacks and she wasn't sure who was more eager, him or her.

His briefs came off and he stood before her like a stone god, his muscles still perfectly formed, though he was a fuller version of the boy she knew in years past, he was now incredibly sexy and so sure of himself. He excited her. His full thick cock stood at the ready and she couldn't wait for him to enter her because she remembered the feeling of him filling her and it was simply perfection.

Wiggling out of her pants she quickly tucked her thumbs into the waistband of her panties and pushed them down her legs, now almost panting with excitement.

"Spread your legs, Red, show me."

She did as he asked and was greeted with a sexy smile.

"Simply perfection." He husked out and then his fingers toyed with her curls, at first lightly brushing them, which caused her to squirm, then firmer as he parted her folds, dipped his forefinger inside of her and spread her juices along the outside and around her clit. She couldn't stop the moan that escaped her throat and his grin told her he liked that. Dipping his finger in again he slid in and out a few times, each time going in deeper and pulling out only slightly.

His wet fingers toyed with her clit, adding pressure as she squirmed, "Show me your boiling point, Red."

She moved her hips so his fingers found that perfect spot and he began manipulating her clit in earnest, sending her spiraling out of control and finally crying out her orgasm.

Before her eyes opened, he climbed over her, both of his legs between hers. "That was fantastic. You should see your face when you cum, Red, it's stunning."

He positioned his cock at her entrance while looking into her eyes. Her legs raised to wrap around his waist and he grinned. "Now, I'm going to watch you again while I cum."

He pushed inside of her and the feeling was glorious.

She felt full and the sensations as his cock filled and pulled out and filled her again sending shivers down her arms and legs. They were a perfect match size wise and after a few thrusts he ground himself against her swollen clit and her eyes rolled back it felt so fantastic.

He chuckled and she opened her eyes to see he was still watching her, and his pace increased. His thrusts grew firmer, and if possible, he went in deeper. His left arm moved down to under her right leg, lifting her slightly and she felt him seat himself fully inside of her and she moaned. She thought he said "yes" but she couldn't be sure where his voice began and hers did. They were in unison, both of them breathing heavily, both of them working to give the other pleasure while achieving it for themselves, too.

"I'm close, Red, come on."

His thrusts now showed his eagerness to climax and she moved her hips so he hit her clit in the perfect way. It only took a few thrusts and her head flew back as she moaned her climax and he thrust once more and let his release flow. A few small thrusts later they were both spent, and their heavy breathing lulled her to a blissful sleep.

## 19

Sliding the pizza he'd just made into the oven, he set the timer then pulled two beers from the refrigerator. He'd done it, he'd lost his heart to Red again. This time it would likely hurt more when she left. He heard his shower shut off and knew she'd be out soon, just in time to eat, then they'd likely just chill. They still had some evidence to look over and hopefully they'd call it an early night. The brief nap they'd taken a while ago would only last for so long.

His phone rang and he pulled it from his pocket.

Glancing briefly at the read out, he answered, "Hey Jared, what have you found?"

Red walked out of the bedroom, her long red hair damp from the shower but she looked fresh faced and happy. Relaxed and satisfied. Damn, he loved that look on her.

"So, for some reason Maggie's kid's birth records are sealed. Why does someone do that? My thinking is baby daddy is married."

"That's what I figured with all the secrecy."

"Yeah, so anyway, I'll keep digging, I've got a couple other ideas, just giving you an update."

"Thanks, Jared." The line was already dead before he got the words out of his mouth.

Red came into the kitchen, a soft smile on her face and he handed her one of the beers he'd just opened. Her warm fresh smelling body pressed against his and her lips landed on his in a soft wet kiss. When she pulled away his lips tingled.

"So, no news?"

"Naw, just that the baby's birth records are sealed, but he's still working on it."

He turned and saw that he hadn't wiped the light dusting of flour from making the pizza crust off the counter and grabbed the dish cloth off the sink. Wiping a swath through the flour, he pulled open the door that held the waste basket and swept the flour into the basket.

Alice exclaimed, "That's it. That's what's been bugging me."

A quick glance saw her staring at the counter. He stopped wiping and waited for her to continue.

"It's been bugging me since we were at the Limitless building. Now I know what it is. By two of the dock doors the dust on the floor had been disturbed. Like the loading docks are still being used. Did you notice that?"

"No, I didn't notice that, I was looking around for crates with drugs in them."

"Well they aren't going to leave that laying around, and since you called Maggie earlier to inquire, there was time for anything to be moved, except a stack of folders in the big office upstairs and whatever it was that Delhurst picked up and tossed in the garbage can. Everything else was pristine. Too pristine for an empty building."

He watched her mind working and it was a marvel. "Don't you think they'd keep it clean for showings?"

Her nose scrunched a bit before she replied. "Maybe, but the loading docks are just that. Industrial and I've been in a ton of buildings, Ace, they're usually not so clean."

"Okay. I'm following."

"So, Maggie calls whoever from the Santarino family hired her and says, 'We have a showing today, and the party is pre-approved.' Then, whoever is still using the building runs over quickly and removes anything they don't want the party to see. Could we be lucky enough to have cameras in the area?"

"I can check but Limitless is out there by itself and we can't record private property without permission."

"How about truck rental places or a warehouse where large trucks are stored. Something that could move large quantities."

"How large do you think these shipments are?"

"Usually it's not the drugs they need all the space for. Drugs are shipped inside coffee cans and other aromatic substances to throw off the drug sniffing dogs. They are often transported with other products to mask their detection They're also packaged smaller and placed into boxes and crates here and there. I made a big bust a couple of years ago and the drugs were wrapped up tight, stuffed into balloons, tied, and then tucked in olive jars."

"Let me make a couple of calls." He was still holding his phone from Jared's call, so he tapped the Captain's name and waited. Alice walked into the living room and stared blankly out the window, but he knew her mind was working.

"Captain, do we have cameras anywhere near the Limitless building?"

"The closest place we have is the convenience store a half mile down the road."

"Can you have someone check it for any large trucks coming or going around the Limitless building this afternoon after you got me the bank pre-approval so I could go in as a potential buyer?"

"I'll have Callan check it out and give you a call."

"Thanks, Captain."

He ended the call and walked to the office to check on trucking companies in the area. He could hear Red's footsteps going upstairs and he chuckled to himself, she was restless.

His internet browser began populating the area trucking companies, most of which weren't actual trucking companies at all, but had used the keywords in their ads to manipulate searches. As he scrolled through, one larger company jumped out at him as he remembered they'd had financial issues last year, and he wondered if they were still in business. Rush Trucking was located on the outer edge of town on the way to Indianapolis. It wouldn't surprise him if they resorted to hauling illegal substances to save their company, and because of their location, no eyebrows would be raised as they headed in that direction out of town. But they'd be running to Indy and likely other stops in between. Which reminded him to ask Red if there were towns between Lynyrd Station and Indianapolis that were also experiencing a surge of drug activity.

Her footsteps sounding on the stairs as she ran down them, as if she were in a hurry. Her head popped around the door and she said, "I've got to go back, Ace. You don't have to come if you don't want to, but I have to go."

"Wait, Red. It's dangerous and you'd be breaking and entering."

"Maybe, but I have a sneaking suspicion about something, and I just have to check it out."

He stood and walked to her, his hands landed on her shoulders, "Don't jeopardize the investigation, Red."

"I won't. I've done this before. I'll go in and satisfy my hunch, then sneak out and figure out a way to get back in there with a warrant. And, if there are people around and I see something, maybe I'll get lucky."

"Not if you're trespassing."

"Then, as you said before, a broken window just may get us what we need to go in and thoroughly search."

"I'll tell you what, if there's a trucking company they're using, we'll find a way to stop and search one of the trucks once they leave the property."

She kissed him quickly as she laughed. "Now you're talking big guy!"

He followed her from the office and grinned at the excitement in her voice. Turning the oven off and grabbing his keys from the cupboard, he followed her out to the garage and hopped in the car. They were officially investigating and no doubt breaking and entering, but it was the closest he'd felt to a solution to this catastrophic drug problem since it had started again shortly after the Santarinos were killed. And, as he backed his car from the garage the weirdest thought crossed his mind. Red had always been like this, eager and ready to go into a mission. She had confidence in herself that he hadn't had in himself back then. Did this mean he'd grown up?

## 20

Rory was quiet as they drove, which was fine, she needed the time to prepare herself. Times like this were when her confidence could easily turn into bravado and she could get herself killed. Of course, that would be bad, but what would be worse was to get Rory killed and have to live with it. He wasn't used to this stuff like she was. Indy and her territory were so much larger than Lynyrd Station, not that he wasn't used to making big moves. His training in the Marines had taught him well, and some of the missions they'd gone on during their time in the service reminded her of how strong and true he was. But they were different when it came to things like this. She wanted to blast in and take names, he wanted to think things through and go by the book. Hopefully, they could meet somewhere in the middle. Normally, her fellow DEA agents managed to restrain her gangbuster approach.

Turning down the road that led them to Limitless, she said, "Is there a back way in?"

His head twisted from side to side, then responded. "I can do better than a back way in."

Easing his car down the road he turned on to a lane, which was obscured by brush, over-grown trees and shrubs. He drove slowly a few feet in, then switched his headlights off. The moon was high in the sky which offered them some light, but she struggled to see any sort of driveway or path.

"How do you know where you're going?"

He chuckled, "I used to bring girls back here to park when I was much younger. Years ago, this was the farm-land my great-grandparents owned. As generations passed, the land was sold off and no one takes care of it anymore."

She didn't like hearing that he'd brought girls back here to make out with, but of course it was likely that he'd had plenty of them in his day. She still thought he was the most handsome man she'd ever met.

He stopped the car, turned off the ignition, and they sat in silence for a few moments. Soon her eyes adjusted, and she could see through a copse of trees some lights higher in the sky.

"That's the Limitless building and the lights are lighting the parking lot. But we can make our way on foot to the other side of the building by the loading docks without being seen, hopefully."

"Okay."

As her eyes adapted and the light breeze moved some of the leaves and branches here and there, she could see a bit more of the parking lot and agreed that walking across it would certainly call attention.

"Red, hang tight for a minute."

He reached up to the over-head light and popped the

cover from it. Unscrewing the lightbulb inside, he set it in the cup holder, the cover next to it.

"When you get out of the car, the only thing that will illuminate it is the dash lights for a minute, don't slam your door but close it quickly."

"Here, let's do this."

She shrugged out of her jacket and pushed it onto the dash, covering the lights.

She could see his smile in the darkness of the car, his teeth glistened in the moonlight. He leaned forward and kissed her quickly, then opened his car door and hopped out, quickly pushing it to latch. Following suit, she mimicked his movements.

Walking to the front of the car as soon as she reached Rory, he took her hand and led her through the tall weeds easily and quietly, or as quietly as they could with their feet crunching on the downed brush and branches.

As they turned a corner, she could see the Limitless building come into view, her eyes scanning the area to see if anyone were guarding the perimeter of the building. Looking along the top of the building she didn't see any cameras which was a good sign because they wouldn't want evidence of their illegal activities for others to see. One thing she felt confident about, there was illegal activity going on there, she could feel it. All her years in the DEA told her that.

Nearing the edge of the wooded area they had walked through, Rory crouched down to look the area over. She did the same and surveyed the area around the loading docks. It didn't appear that anything looked any differently than it had earlier today, but she just had to go in. She stood and began making her way toward the back of the building. There weren't as many lights in the back of the building as in front, but there were two shining in the back. Deciding she could stay between them to get to a door just under the closest light to them, she moved that way. She could hear Rory's steps behind her, so she kept going forward. Just before she stepped out of the tall grass concealing their position, Rory tugged at her hand.

Leaning in he whispered, "What's your plan?"

"I'm going inside." From her back pocket she pulled out a lock picking tool she'd used dozens of times. "Then, I'm first going upstairs to see what that stack of files was on the credenza; after that I'm going down to the loading docks to see what I can find down there. The fact that Delhurst picked up a piece of something and threw it away when everything else was spotless tells me someone was a little sloppy."

"You think Delhurst is dirty?"

"I don't know, what do you think?"

He shrugged and shook his head. "I don't know that much about him."

She heard him inhale. "Red, you go upstairs, I'll check out the loading dock. If we split up the work, we won't have to be in there as long, the less time the better."

"Okay." Unable to resist the rush she felt just working with him, she stood up on her toes and kissed his lips, brushing her breasts against his chest which earned her a tight squeeze from him and hard nipples for her. Ending their kiss, she turned and quickly made her way to the building, Rory close behind her.

## 21

Trying not to be impressed he watched as Red made quick work of the lock, then slipped inside the door. He locked it behind them and watched as she made her way to the staircase that would take her up two floors. She didn't look back and part of him felt sadness that her instincts and training took over and he was in second place once again. That is if he'd ever been in first place with her at all.

Pulling his phone out, he switched on the flashlight and began walking to the loading docks to see the dust disturbance Red mentioned earlier. Shining his light on the floor to see what she meant, it did appear as if something had been dragged or pushed to the dock, then slid off into a truck or something else. Not seeing any equipment in the area, no forklifts or pallet jacks, if something was going on here, it was all done by hand.

The second dock door looked the same as the first, a fine line where the dust had been wiped away from the doorway on both sides of the door. He continued walking the perimeter of the room, his footsteps sounding incredibly loud in the vastness of the empty space, the sound bouncing off one cement wall after another magnifying with each bounce. A metal door hidden behind the staircase caught his attention and he remembered seeing it earlier, but for some reason they never went inside. Making his way across the vacant room, he stopped just before the door and listened for any sounds coming from behind door number one. Testing to see if the door was locked, he smiled when the knob turned, and he quietly pulled the door open.

Inside, he stood in a windowless room, and he tested to see if the light switch worked. A harsh, bright florescent light came to life, flickering at first, then dimly staying on. As his eyes adjusted the light slowly became brighter and he looked around to see what this room was.

A metal desk sat against the far wall with an old battered chair pushed in under it, the dark green vinyl ripped at both edges where the chair had been pushed against the desk over the years. Assuming it squeaked, he decided to leave the chair alone and opened the desk drawers on either side; he hoped they didn't make any sound, but he also knew that was likely wishful thinking.

The top right drawer only lightly rubbed against its tracking and was empty, so was the second, and finally the bottom the same as the other two. Moving to the left side, he pulled the drawer open slowly to reveal an empty envelope, three pencils and a smattering of paperclips strewn about. The second drawer held a ruler and an eraser. The bottom drawer was empty. Taking a deep breath and looking around some more, he found a four-drawer file cabinet in the corner with a coffee maker on top of it. Walking to the cabinet he pulled the first drawer out and the coffee maker wiggled a bit. What was strange was an inch of coffee still sitting in the pot, swirled around. Holding his phone light up to the pot, what he noticed was a puzzle. The coffee didn't have a fine coat of mold or film on it which meant it had been made fairly recently. He pulled the pot off the burner and sniffed. It smelled relatively fresh.

Looking around he saw a wastebasket in the corner. Replacing the coffee pot, he wandered over to the waste-basket and saw two coffee cups and a napkin laying in the bottom.

Pulling the first cup from the can, he looked inside and saw only coffee stains, no moisture in the bottom. He'd have to be a forensic expert to know drying times based on room temperature, etcetera, so he dropped the cup into the can and pulled the second cup out. A small amount of moisture sat at the bottom of the cup, but the interesting thing was this one had lipstick on the edge. A woman. And, since the cup still had coffee in the bottom it had been used somewhat recently.

Hearing a noise from what sounded like the first floor, he dropped the cup in the trash can and crept to the door. Listening intently, he could hear his own heartbeat and hoped beyond all reason that what he heard was Red making her way down to him so they could get the hell out of here. He wanted this drug ring sitting behind bars, but he sure didn't want to be sitting behind bars with them. A cop in jail never lasted very long. Not that breaking and entering could get him thrown in jail, but no sense in pushing their luck.

Not hearing any more sounds, he turned off the light, exited the office, closed the door and decided to finish his search of the perimeter of this room before going in search of Red to get home. He listened again wondering what he'd heard upstairs and felt uneasy that Red wasn't on her way down here. Deciding to screw it and go upstairs, the garbage can that Delhurst had tossed something into earlier caught his attention and he walked as quietly as he could to the can, shining his light inside. There were some miscellaneous pieces of paper, mostly brown packing material, a newspaper and something white and shiny.

Reaching inside for the white object, he strained to grasp it at the bottom of the can; he stretched himself out fully, his fingers finally able to grip it. Pulling it from the can, he shined his light on the object and his heart hammered in his chest as realization of what he held flooded his mind. This was big.

---

## 22

This building was eerie in the deep, dark, dead of night, or more accurately after ten at night with no lights on and when you weren't supposed to be inside. But she just had to follow this hunch. The staircase was dark and echoed with each footstep, but she continued upstairs keeping her eyes and ears alert and her focus on getting at those files.

At the top of the stairs, she heard a sound and hesitated. Trying hard to keep her breathing even and steady; she listened for any sounds except that of her own heartbeat. The constant hum of a motor reached her ears and she realized the sound she'd heard before was the refrigerator kicking on. Then she wondered why they'd keep a running refrigerator in an abandoned building.

Easing down the hallway to the room that was the kitchen or break room, she edged her way to the refrigerator, using only the light from her phone to find her way. Knowing full well once the door opened the room would be flooded with light, but then reminding herself that there weren't any windows in this room, she quickly pulled it open to find a couple of food containers on the top shelf and six yogurt containers in the door. Peaking at the food containers she popped the top off one of them and was surprised to see it wasn't old and moldy but looked rather fresh.

Closing the door and glancing around the room once again, she made her way into the hallway and down to the Presidential office to look at those files. Each doorway she passed gave her pause and yet, she knew no one was here other than Rory, so whatever she was worried about was purely her imagination.

Reaching the door to the big office, she slid inside and shone her light on the credenza across the room. Nothing. Those files were gone. Padding across the plush carpeting, she began opening and closing drawers looking for those missing files but each one was empty. Turning to the desk she began checking the drawers and when each of those was empty, she searched the file cabinet on the far wall. It had only been three hours or so since they'd been in here, so either Maggie moved the files or someone else had been inside while she was. Hopefully, they weren't still here. That thought sent chills running down her spine.

Eager to get down to Rory but also wanting to make the most of this B&E, she decided to investigate the other offices along the hallway to see if the files were still in this building.

Hearing a sound from below, she pressed her back against the wall next to the door and took in a deep, slow breath, then let it out slowly to keep herself in check. A few moments passed and no other sounds could be heard, and she convinced herself it was either a furnace or some other system still running within the building. After all, the refrigerator was still on.

Easing out to the hallway she began moving slowly to the staircase, suddenly more eager to leave than to prove a hunch right.

"What are you doing here?"

She turned at the male voice, which sounded familiar, but she couldn't see the person it came from.

"Who's there?"

Her phone held up, she tried to keep her hand from shaking when the man stepped into the light revealing himself.

"Officer Delhurst, what are you doing here?"

"I believe I just asked you the same question."

"Oh, I thought I saw someone in here and came in to investigate."

"Really?" His voice deepened and the look he gave her was anything but friendly. "How did you get in?"

"The door down in the dock area was open."

He took a step toward her and she instinctively backed up. The grin that creased his face reminded her of the cartoon Grinch whose grin slowly spread across his face and looked purely evil.

"What are you doing here, Officer?"

"I got a call that someone was lurking about in here, lights flashing, etc. So, I came in to check it out."

"Oh."

"Did you find anyone in here?"

"No."

"I wonder why you wouldn't call the station and let them know you were coming in?"

"I happened to be in the area and just thought a quick investigation would be prudent. After all, I know you all are working so much overtime and if it was nothing, I wouldn't want to pull anyone off their assignment for a false alarm."

Her heart beat so hard in her chest it was downright painful and she realized how foolish this likely was. Rory was right; sometimes she was simply too impulsive.

Light footsteps could be heard from the staircase, much too light to be Rory's. Delhurst's eyes never left hers, which scared the shit out of her because he wasn't alone. Hopefully one of Rory's friends from the station came along and would be friendlier.

The door from the stairs opened and she stepped aside so her back wasn't to Delhurst, who stood stock still and never took his eyes from her, to see none other but Maggie standing in the doorway.

Looking her up and down, the perusal gave her the creeps and it was then that her brain registered that this was very serious. As in, possibly lose her job, or worse, deadly serious. Every horrible story she'd ever heard from the various DEA agents she'd worked with flooded through her mind and finally ended with where in the hell was Rory? But, if he were still here, he'd surely hear something and come looking for her.

"So, decided to come back and take a look around on your own, Special Agent Alice Tucker, DEA?" Maggie sneered.

Deciding sarcastic would not go well right now, she opted for nothing at all.

"What did she say, Paul?"

"Saw someone was in here."

"Hmm." Maggie walked toward her, still wearing the pencil skirt and heels from earlier today, still dripping in diamonds, still reeking of money.

"What are you really doing here? And, don't lie."

Moving her body as if she were talking with her hands, she tried making her way to the stairs, but Delhurst pulled his gun, "Not another step."

Maggie chuckled and it was sad or maybe pained in some way. "Take her downstairs, the truck is here, she can be discarded just like they did with my man. Toss her in a box and ship her out with the goods. Dump her somewhere where she won't be found for a long time."

Her mind screamed to keep up, but she struggled with it. Her man? Her baby daddy? Discarded?

"Let's go, Special Agent." The sarcasm couldn't have been thicker.

Delhurst used his gun to point to the stairs as she tried running all the odds through her brain. Run, no, he was taller and likely faster than she. Try and trip him? Could work but then again if not, it would be worse. Go along and see if something better came to mind? That's what she had for now and that Rory would intervene and help her along the way. Hopefully, they hadn't found Rory yet. Where was he anyway?

---

## 23

Hiding in the back of the shipping area, Rory watched as the truck pulled up and three men jumped out. Cases of product were hauled out by hand and stacked in three separate areas. The workers seemed to know what each area meant, but he was still puzzling it all together. Once the truck was unloaded, the boxes and crates were opened, and the product unpacked. Coffee cans were pulled from the cartons, another worker opened the cans and pulled packages from inside. They were then sorted and repackaged in smaller boxes with false bottoms and sorted according to zip code based on the zip codes written on the side of each box. No one talked and everyone did what they were supposed to without a word.

He heard footsteps on the metal stairs and peered around the office he'd recently vacated only to see Red coming down the steps, with Delhurst behind her, a gun in her back. Not long after, he saw Maggie coming down behind Delhurst. That's when things clicked for him. Delhurst hid the files from them and threw the cocaine away. He surely knew what it was but didn't want Red or him to see it and acted as if it was nothing. Slowly drawing his gun from his back holster, he calculated who he'd have to shoot first, Delhurst or Maggie or the workers if each was armed and how long it would take him to pull off enough shots to get each of them and not get Red caught in the cross fire. Or get killed himself.

Deciding he had the advantage while they were on the steps, he saw Red turn his way and slightly nod, she was ready and would hit the floor before anyone else could draw and shoot. He aimed for Delhurst and got him in the ribs, knowing instantly he'd punctured his lung at the way he buckled. Red jumped the final two steps down and rolled out of the way, then pulled her gun from her ankle holster. Maggie turned toward him, her eyes evil glints of steel as she followed Delhurst down the steps and he pulled his second gun from his ankle, this one not police issue, and aimed it at her. Before he could get off a second shot, Red shot Maggie in the stomach and then one of the workers who'd pulled a gun. He took care of the other two by simply pointing his gun at them.

"Lay down, on the ground, hands on the back of your heads." He yelled and they quickly dropped to the ground.

Walking to Delhurst, he heard the wheezing and saw the bubbles of blood on his side, but the man's eyes locked on his and he mouthed, "Sorry."

Maggie tried to crawl toward the gun Delhurst had dropped but Red ran to it and kicked it out of the way. Quickly pulling Delhurst's cuffs, she secured Maggie's hands behind her back. Red then pulled her cell phone from her pocket and called it in.

Keeping his gun trained on the two workers, he waited until officers arrived at the scene, at which point he was relieved from keeping them in his sights. As soon as his Captain arrived, he and Red were each taken to separate areas of the building and questioned, he by his Captain.

"What went down here Richards?"

"I won't lie Captain, and if you have to relieve me of my duties, then do what you have to do, but we came in here tonight because we knew something wasn't right about what we saw today and Red had a strong hunch that something was going down. I went along with it because she's smart and good and her senses on things have always been spot on."

"So, you were here illegally, and yet, it worked out, but we have an officer involved shooting, two of them, one a DEA Special Agent; we've got some issues to work through, but, on the good side, I do believe you've cracked this drug ring."

"Red did, Captain."

"Okay, Richards. Get back to the station. Go straight to the station, Tucker can ride with Waters. Don't talk to each other until we're finished with the questioning. Got it?"

"Yes, sir."

Officer Jason Robards came to the scene and gave him a ride to his car. Since they were all shaken at having a dirty cop in their midst very little conversation was going on other than what was necessary. He couldn't stop shaking, likely from the adrenaline and the fact that he saw Red with a gun at her back and the look of pure terror on her face. He'd never get that sight out of his mind and he never wanted to see it again.

Walking into the station, he felt bone tired and figured that Maggie was behind this whole mess. Talk about someone you'd never think would be involved with something like this and what about her kid?

He sat in his office, his mind still not able to process all that had transpired; and he hoped he'd find out the whole story so he could settle back into his life as usual.

He heard commotion and saw Red walking into the station with Waters and Bowers with her. Red seemed shocked and he wanted nothing more than to pull her into his arms and hold her. But they were likely to be here for a long time yet. He took a deep breath and resigned himself to sitting in until the Captain got back and both of their interrogations were finished. Then, he'd hold her all night long. At least for as long as he had, 'cause now that this was likely wrapped up, she'd be heading back to Indianapolis and that promotion she was counting on. It's what she'd worked her whole life for and that was hard to walk away from, and he'd never ask her to, just like before.

## 24

She was so warm and she felt like she had a weight on her, her limbs felt heavy, but so did her eyes. So heavy. Rory's deep, even breathing behind her warmed her neck and she sighed. Nestling her head deeper into her pillow his arms pulled her closer into his body. That's why she was warm, his arms anchored her to him, and it felt so good.

Prying an eye open she saw the sun shining brightly outside, dust particles billowing in the stream of light from the window. She'd discharged her weapon last night, something she hadn't done in a while. She hoped she never had to do it again. That was if she wasn't charged with wrongdoing. Maggie had still been alive when she and Rory came home last night; if she died during the night, she could very well be charged with some lower degree of murder. She had a solid argument of self-defense, or at least in the defense of another, because when she saw Maggie begin to point her gun at Rory, she didn't even wait to see what was going to happen, she just acted. That was her job, to protect the cops. Aside from that, she'd never be able to forgive herself if Rory had been injured or killed. It was entirely her responsibility he had been there at all. Knowing she'd been right did little to ease her guilt. Hopefully, time would be on her side.

Soft lips kissed the back of her neck before his soothing, deep voice whispered, "Did you sleep good?"

"Yes, better than I have in a long time."

"Mmm. Me, too."

His phone rang and with a groan he rolled over to swipe it off the bedside table.

"Yeah."

She listened to his side of the phone conversation knowing it was likely a summons to come into the station. Dreading that it may be someone calling to say that Maggie had died.

"Yeah."

He tapped his phone ending his call then dropped his arm and his phone to the bed.

"We've got to go in for more questioning."

"Okay. I'll get some coffee going. I can't do anything before coffee."

He chuckled and rolled off the bed. "I'll jump in the shower then start breakfast."

She sat up, realized she was naked, saw his shirt laying on the floor next to the bed and tried to remember how they ended their night here, but she couldn't quite remember it. Clearly exhaustion had set in.

Snagging his shirt from the floor she slipped it over her head and walked out to the kitchen. The first thing she noticed was the aroma of freshly brewed coffee and she smiled. Ahh, what a great thing to wake up to. Then she noticed two cups sitting next to the coffee pot. Pouring coffee into the cups she shook her head when one cup of coffee turned a nice caramelly color. He'd already put creamer in it. He must have done all of this last night after she dropped into bed. What a sweetheart. She would miss him terribly.

That thought had her heart dropping into her stomach; she didn't want to go through that again. What she realized was that she loved him, probably never really stopped loving him and dammit why couldn't they make this work?

She sat at the table looking out over the green backyard and the gorgeous flowers outside and thought how ideal this place seemed. What would she do if she lost her job? Did she want this promotion so bad she'd give up a chance at being with Rory? Maybe a baby or two? A house and a dog? She'd identified herself with that job for so long she didn't really know who Alice Tucker was without DEA after her name. What would she do for money? What did she want to do? All she'd ever known was the military and then the DEA chasing major drug traffickers. She'd likely never be able to do anything that wasn't police work. Working retail was definitely out of the question. Working as a waitress, nope. In an office, oh hell no.

"What are you doing?"

"Wondering what on earth I'll do with myself if I lose my job."

He nodded his head and grabbed his coffee from the counter, taking a seat at the table. His fresh scent smelled better than her coffee and that was saying something before she'd even finished her first cup.

"Well for what it's worth, and I have no idea what will happen, but you could always pick up where Big3 left off."

"What's Big3?"

"Ford, Lincoln and Dodge were Big3 Security before

they joined GHOST. So, from what I understand there's still some private investigation work out there available. But I sure hope it doesn't come to that."

Nodding she whispered, "Me, too."

"Get a move on, Red, the Captain just said he wants us at the station ASAP. Let's try and stay on his good side while he's deciding what to do with us. Yeah?"

"Yeah."

She stood and took her cup with her back to the bedroom, picked up her clothing laying around the floor, then headed upstairs where her overnight bag still sat with her toothbrush and makeup waiting for her.

Once they knew what would happen with them, she'd talk to Rory, but she sure hoped he'd bring it up first. Now to shower off yesterday and get ready for today, come what may.

_____

## 25

S itting in his office searching through his computer, Rory's mind raced with possibilities. He'd come in to find out that Delhurst had died during the night, and the Captain had confirmed he'd been dirty the whole time he was here. He was actually planted in the Police Department by none other than the Santarino family. Would they ever be finished with that no-good family?

Callan Waters entered his office. The giant blocked all the sunlight from the outer room, his shoulders barely fit through his door the brute was so built. But he was a good cop and a good friend.

"Richards, Margery Van Steel is still alive; Bowers just got back from interviewing her. He's in with the Captain who wants to see you."

"Where's Red, I thought she was with the Captain?"

"She's pouring herself another cup of coffee."

He shook his head remembering she didn't function well before at least two cups. Her meeting with the Captain must have been tough. He stood and walked to the door just as Red was walking toward him with two cups of coffee. She handed him a cup and whispered, "I'll wait in here for you."

He nodded then made his way to the Captain's office.

Knocking once on the door, the Captain looked up from a report and waved him in. Bowers sat in one of the empty chairs across from the Captain's desk, and Rory took the empty seat next to him.

"Richards, Bowers is here to fill us in on the interview he had with Van Steel.

"Yes, sir."

He twisted in his chair and looked at Bowers.

"As you know there's been a lot of speculation about Van Steel's baby daddy. Turns out, he's none other than Mangus Santarino. Giovanni Santarino set her and the baby up in a lavish lifestyle, but the tradeoff was that she had to help run the drugs through the Limitless building until Giovanni decides it is time to move operations. Giovanni was getting close to ending this operation here, which was why earlier Al was called and asked to a meeting, to discuss payment. He thought if he could get some money from the station or the State or the Federal Government, he'd take it. He was so angry that both of his sons were killed here, he wanted to twist the knife a bit before moving on. Never intending to get caught, of course.

"Who called Red?"

"Delhurst. He lives in one of those Longstone apartments and was watching everything unfold after Sergio Mancuoso was murdered."

"Who killed Sergio?"

"Delhurst."

"Why? Did he know Sergio was working with Red?"

"Yes. They were going to kill Red too if she got in the way. Last night could have gone much differently. Apparently, they were going to call her to come and meet at Limitless later anyway, after they had their shipment sorted and loaded."

"So, Giovanni is still running the family in Lynyrd Station? Is he about finished with all his dirty tactics?"

"Time will tell. The baby will likely stay here with Margery's mother and there could be some ploys on the family's part to try to get custody of whoever has a Santarino baby, but we'll be watching. Also, he's supposedly teaching Mangus' daughter, Francesca the family business and she's about twenty, so we'll definitely work with Homeland Security to keep her out of the country and, hopefully, anyone loyal to the family. "

"Thanks Bowers, Captain. What happens with Red and I now?"

"There'll be an internal investigation and pending that, you're both on desk duty. Tucker can go back to her District Office, but she'll have to come back for hearings. The District Attorney also will investigate to see if any charges will be brought against either of you."

His stomach dropped at the thought of Red leaving and he knew they'd have to talk. He nodded and stood then bowed his head once more and made his way back to his office, dread weighing heavy in his chest.

Red sat at his desk, her feet propped up on a drawer, her eyes looking around the room at the photographs he had hanging on the walls.

"You look comfortable there."

She smiled, "I suppose I am."

He closed the office door and sat in a chair across from

his desk. "Red, what do you want to do? I mean between you and I?"

Her red hair shined under the light from the fixture above, her eyes still held the tiredness they'd had before, but she was still such a beautiful woman.

"What do you want, Ace?"

Swallowing he took a deep breath, "Take a look at my computer."

Her brows furrowed as she stared at him, then she glanced at his computer. She shook his mouse to wake it up and looked at his screen. The furrow between her brows deepened for a moment as she scrolled down the list of houses on his monitor.

"I don't understand, what are you looking at houses for? I thought you loved your house."

"I do, but the biggest problem with my house is that it isn't where you are. So, if you want us to give this relationship a try, I want to do it right this time and I thought I could buy a house in Indy to be with you."

She stared deeply into his eyes, hers a bright green, a color he wanted to stare into for the rest of his life. He saw her swallow, her eyes glistened as moisture gathered, then she took a deep breath and said, "I was just thinking I could get used to living here in Lynyrd Station. This is my last year as a Special Agent, at 37 we have to transfer. Maybe instead of a transfer, I could move here. I think there's a new opening here. And if it's too hard to work together, maybe I'll take over Big3. Depending on what happens with the investigation."

He watched her, she never wavered. "You sure?"

"Yep. You?"

"Yep."

He pulled a quarter from his pocket. "What do you say, heads we stay here, tails we move to Indy?"

She laughed, her head back, her hair moving about like a cloud around her. "Yeah, but make sure it's heads, Ace."

## 26

Al tried catching her breath as she ran down the narrow path leading her from the street to the back of the old laundromat in Lynyrd Station. She never should have taken her eyes off this girl.

Tuning the corner she saw the blonde silky hair billowing out with each step she took and gave herself one last push to catch her. Rory would be so upset if she didn't catch her.

Bolting past the boxes and crates of items sitting behind the town's buildings she sucked air into her lungs and gave it all she had. Lucky for her, a garbage can caught Harley's attention and she stopped to smell the garbage.

"Gotcha, you little minx." She scooped the furry little pup up into her arms and sat on the ground letting her body rest and her breathing return to normal.

Puppy kisses and snuggles made her giggle, even though she had every right to be irritated with this little trouble maker.

Pulling the leash from her back pocket, where she'd

bound it up feeling sorry for Harley as she kept coughing while they walked, she clipped it to Harley's collar. She'd learned her lesson.

Inhaling deeply, sneaking a few kisses from her pup, she stood, and walked back to the car, holding Harley close. That had been a scare enough not to trust the little actress again with the coughing gag she pulled. Too smart for her own good.

Turning the corner around the laundromat, she stopped short when Rory stood at the end of the alley, arms crossed across his broad sexy chest. The stern look on his face told her he wasn't happy with her.

"You let her off her leash again, didn't you?"

"How did you know that?"

"I happened to be coming home for lunch today and saw you running around the corner. I found a spot to park and waited to see if you'd be coming back soon or if I had to go off helping you look for our girl."

"She was coughing again like the leash was too tight."

"It isn't. You can slid your fingers under her collar, right?"

"Yes."

For the first time his lips parted in a smile. "She knows you cave in and let her run."

"I've never had a dog before, I'm new at this."

"Never?"

"Never." She giggled as Harley licked her face again then squirmed to get to Rory. "She's crazy about you."

She and Harley neared Rory and he held out his hands to take the squirming bundle. The look on his face as Harley kissed him as if she couldn't get enough of him. His laugh was beautiful. They were beautiful together and her heart swelled watching them. Just a man and his dog.

"She loves you as much as I do."

His eyes met hers and held. The emotion she saw in them made her heart beat wildly in her chest. All the years wasted between them made her feel wistful.

"Stop thinking about that Red."

"How do you know what I'm thinking about?"

"I can see it in your face. You're feeling bad about all the years we spent apart. We can't keep dwelling on that, we have to look to the future."

He bent over and set his squiggling little pup on the ground; her leash attached to her collar. Harley immediately tugged toward the street where their cars were parked.

Rory took her hand and kissed her lips. "I love you."

Inhaling deeply she said, "I love you too."

Pulling her toward the street she went willingly reminding herself to stop dwelling.

Rory glanced over at her, "Before we go home, mind if we stop at the station and show off Harley?"

"Not at all. Don't you think they've seen her enough?"

"Nope."

His smile was genuine. He was a happy man. Hopefully, it was largely to her credit, but Harley certainly gave him immense joy.

He walked her to her car and just holding his hand was a thrill. They were out in public and an official couple. Life was pretty good.

Opening the driver's door for her, he waited for her to get in, then he leaned in and kissed her lips as Harley tried jumping in the car, her little paws scratching at her legs. She giggled and so did Rory.

"She's a busy little gal." He whispered.

"Yes, she sure is. You got her?"

"Yeah Red, I've got her. See you in five minutes."

He reached down and scooped Harley into his arms, stepped back and closed her door. She watched as he walked ahead a few car lengths and tucked Harley into the kennel he had in the backseat of his Charger so she'd ride safely. They both had kennels in their cars, where would they put a car seat if they were lucky enough to ever have a baby?

She shook her head so the melancholy didn't slid in, started her car and watched Rory pull away from the curb. Looking behind her to make sure it was safe to pull out, she eased her vehicle onto the road behind Rory's car.

The sun was bright today, the air smelled fresh and she rolled her windows down enjoying the wind swirling around inside the car. She had grown to love Lynyrd Station these past four months. She'd met Rory's friends and some of the wives of the cops at the station and next week she was taking over Big 3 Security from Ford and the guys. Rory remained lead Detective at the Department, at least for now and she had decided working for herself sounded like a great next step in her life.

Turning into the police station parking lot, she parked alongside Rory's car and smiled at Harley's sweet little face staring at her from the back window. Gawd she was adorable.

Getting out of her car she stood just in front of the door watching Rory pull Harley from her kennel, attached her leash to her collar, then set her on the ground and walked toward her.

She moved to open the door, but he leaned forward first and grabbed it, holding it open for her. It always gave her a bit of a thrill. He winked at her and she couldn't help the smile that spread across her face. Dang.

The front of the police station was quiet at this time of day, which was good. After all the activity of the Santarino drug operation and all the wind down that had happened from that, it was pleasant to see people working at a steady pace rather than the fury of the past. Sarah, the receptionist looked up from her computer and smiled.

"Hi Al, how are you?"

"I'm great Sarah, how are the kids these days?"

The pretty brunette pursed her lips and shrugged. "Still busy as ever, but I couldn't love them more." She looked at Rory and nodded. "Hey Rory."

"Sarah, all the guys in the back?"

"Yep."

Sarah looked down at Harley and smiled. "Hey Harley girl, how are you?"

Harley wagged her tail furiously and Sarah shook her head. "That one must get away with everything, she's too cute."

Rory replied as he held the door to the back open for her. "You have no idea."

She led the way around the corner and to the back where Rory's office was and where the other detectives and cops milled about. Many greetings were exchanged and she had to admit she enjoyed these guys but she didn't miss being in a police station every day. That thought really hit home. Then, all of a sudden things got very quiet.

She looked around and they were all staring at her with weird grins on their faces. She looked down to make sure her shirt wasn't askew or that, heaven forbid she had some weird wardrobe malfunction going on. Seeing nothing she looked over at Rory, who smiled at her, then dropped down to one knee.

"Red, all those years ago I met you, fell in love with you and then lost you. I don't want to lose you again." He pulled a shiny orb from his front pocket and held it out to her. "Red, will you marry me?"

She stared into his eyes and so many thoughts collided together. He'd planned this. He loved her all those years ago. He wanted to marry her.

Stupid tears flooded her vision as Rory melted into a watery blur and the silence of the room unnerved her. Harley jumped up on her legs getting her attention and she blinked rapidly, then swiped at her eyes quickly.

Her head bobbed up and down and she swallowed the lump in her throat and said, "Yes."

Taking her left hand in his he slid the gorgeous sparkling ring onto her finger, kissed it, then stood and planted the biggest kiss on her lips as his arms wrapped her into the best hug she'd ever felt. Life was a thing of beauty and she'd met her match in Rory Richards.

# SNEAK PEEK

The End of **Rory:Finding His Match**.

    Get Defending Keirnan, GHOST Book One now.

Continue reading for a Sneak Peek at Defending Keirnan, the first book in the exciting GHOST Series.

## DEFENDING KEIRNAN, GHOST
## BOOK ONE

T urning the corner and entering the back section of the library, which was closed off to the general public, Keirnan frowned at the condition of this part of the gorgeous historical building downtown. She'd been organizing the program, *Read with Your Littles*, for well over two years. At first it was difficult getting busy parents to take another hour or more out of their already busy weeks to bring their little children to the program; but it became an occasion to spend time together reading and talking about the stories and enjoying each other's company.

But, her patience had paid off, and parents began pouring in. There were children with a single parent; some parents worked long or odd hours. So, she had encouraged not only parents but grandparents to join in, even babysitters. Low and behold, her small project, Read with Your Littles, began filling up. They'd grown to capacity at the Beachwood Elementary School library. So, after only one year, she'd received permission from the Friday Harbor Town Council to move the venue to the

downtown library. As generous as it was that the town had
been eager to accept Keirnan Vickers' program, this old
library building was in poor shape.

Many windows had been painted closed, which was a
safety hazard. The handrails on the steps were loose, the
flooring was sadly neglected and the plumbing, well the
plumbing, was atrocious. That's when she knew she had
to do something. The town had agreed to pay the lion's
share of the repairs, but Keirnan had to first raise dona-
tions to cover the first one quarter of the $500,000 repair
costs.

With the help of her best friend and fellow teacher,
Lexi, she organized a huge fundraiser to the detriment of
her sleep. Did she invite the right people? Would they
come with money, credit cards or checkbooks in hand to
donate? Would the library be able to make many of the
necessary repairs? Or would she look the fool? It was the
last one that kept her awake into the wee hours of the
morning.

Hearing a loud bang, she stopped and turned. Waiting
to hear more or someone moving around, she hesitated to
go investigate. The library was open now, but this wing
was not. She was simply keeping her decorating stash
here so she could bring it in small batches and not have to
haul in carload after carload.

Another bang had her heart racing and the tiny hairs
on the back of her neck prickling. Inhaling deeply, she
slowly walked down the hallway and in the direction of
the noises.

"Hello?" Waiting for a response, she could only hear
her heartbeat thrumming in her ears. Swallowing, she
called a bit louder. "Is anybody back here?"

Looking into the first room, grateful the sun was still

high in the sky, she didn't see anything but stacks of chairs on top of tables that had seen better days and bags of decorating supplies: pretty purple hanging decor, napkins, matching plastic wear and expensive looking, but not, plastic plates for guests at the fundraiser. She had wrestled with how fancy to make the event, opting for low budget, showing their future benefactors that they wouldn't be squandering their money on needless frilly things.

An old portrait of Mr. Vandebrooke, the founder of the town and this library, hung askew on the far wall. The eerie look on his face, that vacant look that signified the artist was not quite able to capture the soul of the man, just the body, gave her the chills. Did his eyes follow her? Shaking her head, she chastised herself for her overactive imagination.

Turning to the hallway once again, she ventured down it further to the next door. "Hello?"

From the corner of her left eye she thought she saw movement. Jumping and stifling a squeal she looked to her left and surveyed the area. What did she just see? Nothing seemed out of place, then again, how would she know? She rarely came back this far other than to make lists of the things that needed upgrading. Another sound came further down the hallway.

Her heartbeat increased further, and her hands began to shake. She'd never been one to scare easily, and she'd seen her share of old buildings in her twenty-five years; it was likely a mouse or a broken window allowing the breeze to move items on the wall or a door closing. She continued to the next room and jumped about a foot off the floor when she saw a man sitting in a chair in the far-left corner of the room. She'd never seen him before, not in town or in the library, but he seemed as if he was waiting for her to appear.

"Hello. May I ask what you're doing in this wing?" Proud her voice didn't shake proving her fright.

"I'm a potential investor in this great building and wanted to see for myself during the day just how bad the condition is."

Swallowing to moisten her dry throat she forced a smile. "Oh, I'm Keirnan Vickers, one of the fundraisers. I'm happy you've taken such an interest in the building and that you can see for yourself the poor condition it's in."

"Yes. That's clear as day."

"What is your name, please?" The way he stared at her made her skin crawl. The close to being a sneer on his face kept her from coming any further into the room.

"That's not important. I'll be on my way in just a moment."

"But, I don't think anyone is supposed to be in this area, Mr. ?"

"But then again, here you are as well." He stood and she guessed his height as just under six feet. His sandy-colored hair was slicked back, and tied together at his nape in a short ponytail. He wore a clean, dark blue, short-sleeved, three-button, placket shirt, jeans and sneakers. He didn't look like someone who had the money to invest, but a person could never know for sure.

"Yes, I'm storing some of the items for the fundraiser in this section to keep them out of the way."

His hands tucked into the front pockets of his jeans, he began walking around the room, first looking at the windows, then at a photograph on the wall. As he neared her, she straightened her back fighting the urge to turn and run. If he actually was a benefactor, it was imperative that she leave him with a positive impression.

"Well, I'll see you in two weeks at the fundraiser then, Mr.?"

He inhaled deeply, removed his hands from his front pockets, and walked to the door as if ready to leave. She stepped aside and swallowed. Clamping her hands together in front of her, she hoped she didn't look as scared as she felt. His whole demeanor seemed bizarre at best.

He walked to the door, then stopped in the doorway, turning to look at her. His eyes stared into hers for a long moment before trailing down her body. The dreadful feeling that plummeted to the pit of her stomach left her ready to run screaming from the room.

He simply smiled, though it looked scornful. He nodded as if dismissing her and left the room.

Allowing herself a moment to regain her composure, and let her knees stop shaking, she inhaled and exhaled a few times, nodded her head and began walking as quickly as she could to the main area of the library to tell, Bekah Dodson, the curator, that someone was in the closed section. Her skin crawled again and she looked back and forth into the rooms to make sure he wasn't going to jump out at her or follow her. She chastised herself for being a scaredy-cat, but he was a creepy-ass man. The first thing she'd do is ask Lexi, if she had added to the guest list.

\*\*\*

This concludes your Sneak Peek at Defending Keirnan, the GHOST Prequel. Grab your copy now to continue reading about Dane and Keirnan.

Available at www.PJFiala.com

## ENJOY THIS BOOK? YOU CAN MAKE A BIG DIFFERENCE

Reviews are the most powerful tools in my arsenal when it comes to getting attention for my books. As much as I'd like to, I don't have the financial muscle of a New York publisher. I can't take out full page ads in the newspaper or put posters on the subway.

(Not yet, anyway.)

But I do have something much more powerful and effective than that, and it's something that those big publishers would die to get their hands on.

**A committed and loyal bunch of readers.**

Honest reviews of my books help bring them to the attention of other readers.

If you've enjoyed this book I would be so grateful to you if you could spend just five minutes leaving a review (it can be as short as you like) on the book's vendor page. You can jump right to the page of your choice by clicking below.

Thank you so very much.

# ALSO BY PJ FIALA

Click here to see a list of all of my books with the blurbs.

## Contemporary Romance
### Rolling Thunder Series

Moving to Love, Book 1

Moving to Hope, Book 2

Moving to Forever, Book 3

Moving to Desire, Book 4

Moving to You, Book 5

Moving Home, Book 6

### Second Chances Series

Designing Samantha's Love, Book 1

Securing Kiera's Love, Book 2

## Military Romantic Suspense
### Bluegrass Security Series

Heart Thief, Book One

Finish Line, Book Two

Lethal Love, Book Three

### Big 3 Security

Ford: Finding His Fire Book One

Lincoln: Finding His Mark Book Two

Dodge: Finding His Jewel Book Three

Rory: Finding His Match Book Four

**GHOST**

Defending Keirnan, GHOST Book One

Defending Sophie, GHOST Book Two

Defending Roxanne, GHOST Book Three

Defending Yvette, GHOST Book Four

Defending Bridget, GHOST Book Five

## GET A FREE EBOOK!

Building a relationship with my readers is the very best thing about writing. I send monthly newsletters with details on new releases, special offers and other fun things relating to my books or prizes surrounding them.

If you sign up to my mailing list I'll send you:

1. A copy of Moving to Love, Book 1 of the Rolling Thunder series.

2. A book list so you know what order to read my books in.

You can get Moving to Love **for free**, by signing up at https://landing.mailerlite.com/webforms/landing/n1o3i7

## MEET PJ

PJ is the author of the exciting Rolling Thunder series, Big3 Security, Second Chances, GHOST series and Bluegrass Security series. Each of these series feature page turning military alphas and the women who love them.

Her online home is https://www.pjfiala.com.
If you prefer to email, go ahead, she'll respond - pjfiala@pjfiala.com.